WHO KNOCKS?
MAGAZINE

An unearthly magazine celebrating the other worldly, the ghostly, the mysterious and the strange.

I warned you not to open the door...

Issue #1

Managing Editor: Krystal Lawrence
Associate Editor: Alton Price

For comments or to submit stories:
Who Knocks Magazine
editor@WhoKnocks.net

www.WhoKnocks.net

ISBN: 978-1-948046-48-0 (ebook)
ISBN: 978-1-948046-49-7 (paperback)

Cover Images
iStock Photo: 136736444, 177415910
Interior Images
iStock Photo: 155357806, 451273897, 524232495, 499678577, 882063322, 915162252, 1057757968, 612261938

Contributors:

Forrest Brazeal
Frank Oreto
Carl Hughes
Dennis Warren
Ken Kreps
Catherine Turner
Kellen Blair
Jay Seate

20190212

Letter From the Editor
Welcome to *Who Knocks?* Magazine

Dear Reader,

It is with my sincerest thank you that I write this letter. We have been both overwhelmed and humbled by the interest in Who Knocks? from writers and readers alike. The support has made releasing this first issue even more gratifying for all of us. So, whether you have downloaded the digital version or are holding the hard copy in your hands, our goal is to give you a story-telling journey that makes time stand still. We set out to be a place that celebrates the otherworldly, the ghostly, the mysterious and the strange. And I believe the collection of finely crafted tales we have assembled in this issue from some tremendously talented writers will do just that.

In coming issues we plan to expand our horizons to include a true crime corner as well, because I have learned that sometimes truth is indeed stranger than fiction. If you have any other suggestions for things you would like to see in future issues, a guest-blog, or just comments about the current issue, we welcome your thoughts and ideas. We might even publish them. Please email all correspondence to editor@whoknocks.net

Thanks to Steve Himes with Telemachus Press for making this magazine a reality. Without you, Steve, there would be no us. We couldn't have done it without your generosity, expertise and guidance.

To all who read this magazine; We wish you a magical 2019, filled with laughter, love, and stories that scare you enough to sleep with the light on.

Warmest wishes,
Krystal Lawrence
and the Staff of Who Knocks?

The following is a message to all the writers who took the time to send us your story for consideration:

We appreciate you so much! As a new magazine, we were taken by surprise when we received hundreds of submissions from authors all over the world. We are a magazine run by writers. As such, we understand the energy, time and love poured into crafting a tale. For this reason, I truly wish that we could have published each and every story we received. If you submitted a story for our consideration that wasn't a good fit, I urge you to keep trying. Keep sending us and other publications your work until you find a home. There is a lock for every key.

We have many stories in the queue that we haven't reviewed yet, so please be patient with us if you are waiting for a response. We are reading the stories that were entered into our writing contest first, and then moving on to general submissions. The $250 winner of our contest will be announced on March 15th. Check our website to see all the goodies we are giving away to the grand prize winner, and pick up the next issue to see the featured author and story. Thanks to all who have entered. We will continue to accept stories for the contest through March 7th.

WK

In this Issue:

Author Spotlight:

This month Canadian author:
  William Blackwell   1

Featured Stories:

Author Spotlight

A candid interview with dark fiction author William Blackwell

Canadian author William Blackwell studied journalism at Calgary's Mount Royal University and English literature at Vancouver's University of British Columbia. He worked as a print journalist for many years before deciding to pen dark fiction novels in 2012. He has written over seventeen novels.

His titles include *Brainstorm, Nightmare's Edge, The Rage Trilogy, Assaulted Souls Trilogy, Orgon Conclusion, Rule 14, Resurrection Point, The Strap, A Head for an Eye, Blood Curse, Black Dawn, The End Is Nigh, Freaky Franky, The Dark Menace,* and *The Witch's Tombstone.*

 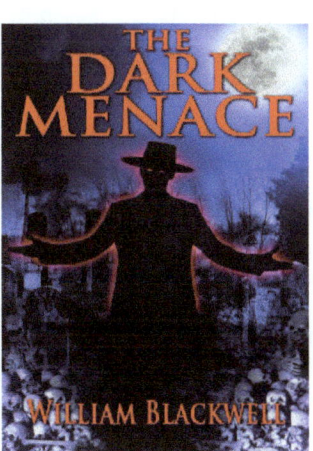

Although he writes predominantly horror novels, Blackwell has dabbled in other genres including sci-fi, psychological thriller, dark thriller, inspirational fiction, post-apocalyptic fiction and paranormal. His work has been characterized as raw, gritty, and real.

Blackwell lived in Vancouver for many years, where he studied his craft and honed his skills. He also lived in Calgary for over a decade, where he began his journalism career. Currently he lives on a secluded acreage on Prince Edward Island and travels often to third-world countries where he finds inspiration for many of his books. He loves to travel, and live life on the raw fringe of society.

Blackwell writes first to feed his addiction and satisfy his need to create. He also writes to "educate, influence, entertain, and scare the hell out of you."

We recently sat down with William Blackwell for a candid interview. Here is a rare glimpse into a strange, prolific, dark and creative mind.

WK: What motivated you to start writing in this genre?

BLACKWELL: More than anything, my nightmares motivated me to start writing horror and dark fiction novels. As far back as I can remember, I've had nightmares, many so terrifying they jolted me awake, terrified and sweat-soaked. They seemed so real at times that I started writing them down in a journal. Many of them became the seeds for my novels. Often my nightmares occur during a work in progress and end up forming an entire chapter or a key element of the story I'm telling. Incorporating my nightmares into my novels has become a therapeutic exercise, as well as providing entertainment, chills and thrills for my readers.

WK: What authors have inspired your work and which are your favorite authors?

BLACKWELL: Horror master Stephen King,

one of my favorite authors, influenced me a lot. I love *The Stand*, his Bible of post-apocalyptic fiction. Dmitry Glukhovsky, author of post-apocalyptic thriller *Metro 2033*, inspired my *Assaulted Souls* series. I also enjoy reading books by Michael Crichton, Clive Barker, John Grisham, Dean Koontz, Sidney Sheldon, H.P. Lovecraft, and Douglas Preston, to name a few.

WK: What was the first book you read that ever made you cry?

BLACKWELL: I don't remember, but there have been a few. My writer friend Sharon McKay recently gifted me *The End of the Line*, a young adult fiction novel. Sharon travels to war-torn countries and writes gripping fiction novels about strife and suffering. Her style is very compelling and powerful and one scene in *The End of the Line* in which a character dies had me teary-eyed and running for the Kleenex.

WK: What do you think are the most common traps aspiring writers fall into? What advice would you give to avoid them?

BLACKWELL: One of the most common traps aspiring writers fall into is not promoting themselves. As an indie author, I think one of my biggest mistakes in the beginning was not concentrating on promotion. I used to just churn out novel after novel with the mistaken belief that the sheer volume and quality of work would separate me from the sea of mediocrity. Not true. To succeed in this business, you have to be more than a great writer. You also have to be a great marketer.

WK: What do you think is the best cure for writer's block?

BLACKWELL: In two words, keep writing. I very rarely suffer from writer's block. But when I find myself stalling and the prose becoming a little wooden, the dialogue stilted, I write through it. Normally I find that as my mind becomes immersed in the story, the sentences become smooth, clear and concise. Since I edit

my work ad nauseam, I know I can return to the clunky bits and polish them up later.

WK: Do you think someone can be an effective fiction writer if they don't feel emotions strongly?

BLACKWELL: I think to convey emotions in a powerful and compelling way, you need to feel them in much the same way. If an author fails to experience emotions strongly, his or her story would probably come off as contrived.

WK: Have you ever based a fictional character on a real person?

BLACKWELL: I've never based a fictional character entirely on anyone I knew. However, I have combined elements of different people to make a unique and interesting character. One such character is Franklin Reiger, an antagonist in my horror novel *Freaky Franky*. Although it seemed unlikely at the time, Franky has become one of my favorite characters. What makes a horror novel interesting is when characters are not black and white. Shades of gray are what encourage readers to identify with them.

WK: What kind of research do you do, and how long do you spend researching before beginning a book?

BLACKWELL: It depends on the book. When I started *The Dark Menace*, I spent over three months researching string theory and the notion of ten dimensions and alternate realities. I also studied Shadow People, the Hat Man phenomenon, and sleep disorders such as sleep paralysis, somnambulism, sexsomnia, and lucid dreaming. The result is a bizarre supernatural thriller—slated for release in about three months—about a nightmare-plagued man who suspects an enigmatic doctor may have unleashed a torrent of horrifying attacks by the Shadow People and the Hat Man.

WK: What's the most difficult thing about writing characters of the opposite sex?

2

BLACKWELL: When writing female characters, I take great pains not to sound sexist. Nor do I want the woman to be portrayed in an exploitative manner or characterized as an object. I have a female editor and two female beta readers who are quick to set me straight if they find me straying in any way, shape, or form.

WK: Of all the characters you have created, who is your favorite and why?

BLACKWELL: I have many favorites. One of them is Doctor Neil Samuelson, from *The Dark Menace.*

WK: What do you like about Doctor Samuelson?

BLACKWELL: I find him interesting and intriguing because of his motivation. His wife of over thirty years passes away and he dedicates the rest of his life to trying to find a means to travel to another dimension, where he believes she is. But his purpose is twofold. He also believes this dimension holds the key to saving humanity. Such dedication and hard work motivated solely by love is hard to resist. It makes him very real, very vulnerable, and one of my all-time favorite characters.

WK: William, thanks so much for taking the time to speak to us. Do you have any closing remarks?

BLACKWELL: You're very welcome. I'm really excited about *The Witch's Tombstone*, my latest work in progress. It involved extensive research on legends of witches who reportedly lived on Prince Edward Island during the 17th century. One such which was falsely accused of witchcraft, convicted, and burned at the stake. I expect *The Witch's Tombstone* to be released in about six months. Here's a short synopsis to whet your appetite:

Chelsea McGuinness is saddened and disappointed when her husband Taylor Madden takes her to a cemetery on the evening of their two-year wedding anniversary. But he calms her down, assuring her the witch's tombstone is nothing more than folklore and myth—a joke really.

However, her experience is anything but a joke. She sees the apparition of a young woman resembling herself, hears a desperate cry for help, and for a terrifying moment becomes catatonic with panic and fear.

Soon after, strange things start happening. Chelsea develops shadowy supernatural powers and her friends begin behaving erratically. A stranger in a bar savagely attacks her with a broken bottle, trying to slit her throat. Her home mysteriously disappears down a powerful sinkhole.

As events spiral out of control, Chelsea learns she's the descendant of a witch who was burned at the stake in the 1700s for her crimes. Worse still, she believes a psychotic preacher is brainwashing his congregants and spearheading a modern-day witch-hunt designed to purge society of his twisted version of blasphemy and evil.

As grisly murders and natural disasters ravage Prince Edward Island, Chelsea joins forces with an unlikely band of followers. She's plunged into a fight for her life and a desperate battle to prevent one of her worst nightmares—the coming of a devastating apocalypse.

WK: Check out our next issue for another Author Spotlight interview...

3

GHOST RUNNERS
by Forrest Brazeal

FOUR OF THEM disappeared: all in the same afternoon, all baseball players, all varsity. Two were pitchers. Gabe Lewis was the backup catcher, squat-shaped, the hairiest man in tenth grade. Johnny Alamogordo dominated at every position on the diamond.

Coach A told us the next day at practice, though we didn't actually practice. "Somebody saw them hiking up to the reservoir." His voice was husky and remote, his eyes red-blown. Johnny was his son. "They have divers out there now. If you know anything … if you've heard or seen …"

I couldn't listen. My stomach hurt. I didn't know how the boys had disappeared, and I didn't want to know. But I knew what the four

of them had in common: Adam Ritchie.

I found Adam in his usual spot during varsity practice: parking his butt on the edge of the meager bleachers, scribbling in a five-pocket notebook. A big-headed, soft-bodied kid with plastic-frame glasses that slipped and slid eternally on his tiny nose. My cleats crunched in the gray-packed dirt as I approached him. "Hey."

He looked up with wide fast-blinking eyes and scrambled a couple of rows higher on the bleachers. His discount store sneakers rang against the metal. "What?"

"Settle down. I just want to talk to you."

He stared at me, waiting, making no encour-

4

aging sign.

"My name's Justin," I said.

"I know."

"I noticed you like to sit here and watch."

"Yeah." He rubbed the spine of the notebook, as if it held secrets he couldn't decide whether to trust me with. "I like baseball," he admitted finally.

"Cool," I said. "You should try out for JV."

He squirmed and looked away. I remembered how Gabe and Johnny used to try and foul off batting practice in his direction, and Adam's uncoordinated flopping motions when a ball sailed too close. "Or you could go to a batting cage," I hedged.

His eyes rolled over, flat and filmy, like a dreaming snake's. "In the old days there were kids in every neighborhood who could play," he said as if reciting a litany. "Twenty or thirty kids, all running down to the sandlot every chance they got. Old leather gloves and balls, sticks for bats. Stickball they called it." He shook his head slowly. "It takes a lot of kids to play a real game of baseball."

"I guess so." I glanced backwards—was anyone laughing at me for talking to the weirdo? The field was almost empty. Nobody cared today.

"At home I used to imagine a sandlot full of kids," Adam continued. "I'd bat off a tee and put ghost runners on the bases. But here's the funny part: if we lived in the old days and those kids were really around, I know they wouldn't have wanted me on their team. Even imaginary friends won't play with me."

I half-laughed, picking at my jockstrap. "I'm sure that's not true."

He shrugged and turned back to his notebook. I saw columns of figures: decimal points lined up straight down the page like perforation marks. Batting averages. "You keeping score or something?"

"Kind of."

This was getting nowhere fast. "Hey, listen. I was just wondering ... since you're around so much ... do you know anything about Johnny and them?"

This time I didn't want to meet Adam's eyes. I studied the ground. He made a clicking noise with his pencil against his teeth. "Well," he said after a minute, "I think maybe they got sent down."

Something cold made its way up my legs and settled in the sweaty places of my body. "You mean you ... you think somebody pushed them into the reservoir?"

"No." He shuffled his feet impatiently. "I said sent down, not pushed. You know how when a major leaguer isn't doing so great, he might get sent down to the minors for awhile? That's what I'm saying."

All of a sudden I was tired. This had been a bad idea. "There's no minor leagues in high school, buddy." I started to walk away.

"Well, maybe there should be." He raised his voice for the first time, and the shrill squawk of it in the gray afternoon made me cringe. "Everything's measured in baseball. There's a stat for even the littlest thing. If you're doing bad, everybody knows, and you're off the team. But in life, you do bad and nothing happens. Nothing!"

I ran away from him then, feet pounding in the dust, cleats scarring the foul lines and the sloping pitcher's mound. I ran wind sprints in the crabby outfield grass and tried not to hear Adam's squawking voice.

～✿～✿～✿～

They didn't find the kids in the reservoir. Not with divers or with a net. Rangers with search dogs went into the surrounding Shianna National Forest. After three days they stopped dragging the water, Coach A took leave, and one of the gym teachers from the middle school ran baseball practice.

On the fourth day I went up to the reservoir myself after the intra-squad game, not bothering to change out of my Shianna Hilltoppers uniform. It wasn't a bad hike in the spring, only about a mile from the school, up a collection of stone steps built and broken in the side of a hill. If the weather was nice, you'd find ninth graders making out in the new grass on either side of the path. Today was overcast, not exactly threatening, but the slopes were abandoned. I guess nobody felt like going to second base on Johnny Alamogordo's grave.

The reservoir itself dated from Roosevelt's New Deal: a flat expanse of colorless water reflecting the dead sky. A perfectly spherical cement path surrounding it. A high railing between the path and the embankment leading down to the water: you couldn't fall in here, not by accident anyway. Nobody anywhere in sight.

No, somebody. Adam, on a bench by the path. Still scribbling in his eternal notebook. He heard my cleats on the cement and looked up. "What are you doing here?"

"I don't know."

He stared at me, pencil poised. "But you did know, didn't you?"

I took off my cap and clawed sweat out of my hair. "Knew what?"

"You knew they took me up here. You knew why."

I shook my head rapidly, tasting salt drops. "I didn't believe they would really do it. I thought it was a joke. You know how they are ... how they were."

He smiled crookedly and jabbed his glasses back into place. "I was the stupid one. They told me they would play catch with me up here. I believed them."

I thought of Johnny Alamogordo's face, sun-seared even in March, with the shadow of dark fuzz on the jaw, the bright compelling eyes. If

6

Johnny asked you to do something, you did it, simple as that. Not just to win the implication of his friendship, but because he had a way of forcibly transferring enthusiasm from his brain to yours. Johnny's ideas, good and bad, were viruses.

"They pulled my pants down. Made me do stuff." Adam's voice was as dull as the sky. "They took pictures on their phones."

"I'm sorry," was all I could think of to say. "Really. I should have stopped them. I should have said something."

"A little late," he said. "But it doesn't matter now. They got sent down."

The smooth water drew my eyes again. "They're not in the reservoir, Adam."

"No," he agreed. "They're here." He fished around in the front pocket of his notebook and drew out a handful of colored cards. Baseball cards, homemade with magic markers and a straightedge. Careful block lettering of the names: JONATHAN "JOHNNY" ALAMOGORDO, SHORTSTOP. GABRIEL "GABE" LEWIS, CATCHER. "I've got them all."

He'd hand-drawn the pictures on the cards. He was a surprisingly decent artist—maybe he'd traced photographs. Johnny posed with a bat cocked over his left shoulder. Gabe crouched behind home plate. The pitchers stretched and bowed. Something wrong in each picture. Pinpoints of light in the faces. He'd literally defaced his work with a sharp pencil.

"Adam," I said. "Why are their eyes poked out?"

He shuffled the cards back into the folder. "Doesn't matter."

"No, it does matter. That's super creepy."

He just kept looking at me, his expression flat and torn like the cards. "They couldn't hack it at this level anymore, that's all. Their stats sucked. I had to send them down. It was only fair to the rest of us."

"What did you do to them, Adam?" I whispered.

He drew another card from the folder. Purple ink around the edges with a thin gold stripe—Hilltopper colors. The player on the card was running, skidding with one hand on the ground as if trying to escape a pickle, looking back over his shoulder with wide fearful eyes. When Adam flicked his thumb I saw the lettering on the card: JUSTIN HARRISON, LEFT FIELDER. "I'm sorry, Justin," said Adam. "But I've kept careful track of your statistics and I just think you need to work on some aspects of your game before you can compete here."

I tried to laugh, and didn't like the way it sounded on the flat hilltop. Weren't there supposed to be some rangers around? Why was everything so quiet? "What, you're gonna poke my eyes out too? Is that supposed to scare me?"

"It seems to work," was all he said, and he picked up his pencil and punctured the card with two swift motions: tock, tock.

You know that feeling you get when you stand up too quickly and all the blood rushes to your head? And how, if it's bad enough, your mind can turn upside down, tangled up with the last thought you were having, so that for a second you almost forget who and where you are? That's what happened to me when Adam stabbed the card. I staggered and fell to my knees, but the ground under me was soft, not concrete. The light had changed, like the sun had come out bright. And the cool air on my face was gone.

I wasn't on top of the hill anymore. I crouched on a pitcher's mound. Deep, red dirt stained my knees and clogged up my cleats. Not that orangey Diamond Pro stuff—real bright red, like blood from a fresh cut. Bold white foul lines, fresh-sprayed. A chain link backstop behind me. Out past second base, an outfield with long, weed-tangled grass shading into unfenced distance. The diamond glittered as if under powerful floodlights, but I couldn't see a light source anywhere. Impenetrable darkness surrounded the field on all sides.

"Welcome to the bush leagues, kid," said Adam's voice.

He stood close behind me, an umpire's mask obscuring his face. "Adam," I said, intending to shout but barely able to croak out a whisper. "Get me out of here."

"That's not how it works," umpire-Adam told me. "No shortcuts in baseball. You gotta play your way out of this league. One way or the other."

I grabbed for him, intending to rip the mask off his face. My hand went right through his head and came out clean on the other side, as if I had tried to grab a wisp of fog. He stood unmoving and undisturbed.

The ghostly Adam clicked a little counter in his ethereal hand. "Assaulting the umpire," he said. "I'll overlook it this once, but that's a good way to get suspended."

For the second time in four days I ran from him, across the red dirt and through the waist-high grass in foul ground. I came up hard against a railing, whacking my hip, and stared down into blackness. The faintest glimmer on water.

"Yeah, I put the field in the middle of the reservoir," said a different Adam. "We're in my head, you know. I can do anything here. I have a big imagination." He placed a weightless hand on my shoulder. This version of Adam wore a batboy's unmarked uniform.

Turning around, I saw more Adams taking their places around the diamond, creeping up to the edge of the infield cutouts, squaring off in the on-deck circle, snapping baseballs back and forth in short right field. Their motions fluid and deceptively effortless, major league caliber. In his own head, Adam was a superstar at every position.

"So this is the game?" I asked. "Just you and me?"

"Not quite," replied batboy Adam.

Out of the tall outfield grass trudged three figures, flat-footed, shoulders down. Johnny and the two pitchers. The blood-red dust smeared their uniforms. Johnny hoisted a knotted stick over one shoulder, and the one of the pitchers carried a lumpen leather ball. They took their places around the infield, seeming to barely notice me.

No sign of the hairiest man in tenth grade. "Where's Gabe?" I asked.

Behind the backstop loomed an old-fashioned manual scoreboard, the kind where colored cards represent the numbers of the game. Instead of team scores, the board showed statistics for individual players. ALAMOGORDO. HARRISON. LEWIS. The stats didn't make any sense to me, but I could tell they were mostly zeroes. Gabe's line had been replaced with the word DEMOTED.

"He didn't want to play ball." Batboy Adam shrugged. "He's been sent down to a lower league. And believe me, there are much lower leagues."

I caught a glimpse of Johnny's face: pale and slack-jawed, with none of the old charisma in his eyes. For the first time in his sixteen years, Johnny Alamogordo was out of ideas.

"Please let me go," I said. "Just let me go."

"You're up, Harrison," said umpire Adam, striding briskly to break up our conversation. "There's still time to turn your season around." He slapped me on the back and the clamminess of his touch went straight into my bones. "Play ball!"

Forrest Brazeal is a software engineer, writer, and cartoonist based in rural Virginia. His speculative fiction has appeared in numerous publications. He likes baseball statistics, but he's not creepy about it.

8

DECORATION

By Frank Oreto

THE BLOODY HEAD squelched as Hank forced it onto the spike. He gave it an appraising look. Gruesome enough, but balance was important too. "Hmm, I wish there was someone to hold this up for me."

Voices erupted from behind him. Hank turned to the gaggle of adolescents staring wide-eyed at his house.

"Okay, so who wants to help?"

Hands shot up. He settled on Freddy. A skinny eleven-year-old, almost skeletal enough to pass for a Halloween decoration himself.

Hank handed him the spike and stepped back to the sidewalk. Freddy held the gruesome prop and beamed with pride.

"Oh my God." Freddy's mother joined the group. She was a pretty woman, with high cheekbones and eyes that sparkled with humor. She'd gotten divorced about the same time as Hank but seemed to handle it better.

"Hey, Dianne. You okay with your boy helping out?"

She grinned. "Of course. He loves it. But honestly, Hank, I don't know how you do it.

9

This stuff gives me the willies."

"That's the idea," Hank said. "Right kids?" The children cheered in affirmation.

Hank looked at the spike. "Could you lean it a little to the left, Freddy? Yeah... right there." He had to admit it was a pretty scary effect.

"You know, you got some competition this year," said Dianne.

"Who, Pete Williams down on Maple? He's mostly into hay bales and happy scarecrows."

"No, a new guy over on Beaumont Street— the house that backs on to the ravine. It's not like what you do. It's hard to describe, but the effect is really spooky."

Within moments the crowd of children launched an expedition to this exciting new wonder.

Hank took pity on Freddy. He took the spike and shoved it into the earth. "Catch up with your friends."

Dianne watched her son jog down the street. "Whatever happened to loyalty?"

Hank laughed. "Can't blame them for being curious. You got time for a drink? I got a little red wine, or maybe one of my pumpkin beers. If you're in a seasonal mood."

"Thanks, but I need to get dinner ready." She looked back at Hank's home and gave him an encouraging nod. "It looks good—scary I mean."

Hank took in his handiwork: foam core tombstones, rotting hands thrusting from faux graves. It was good. Fog machines, strobe lights. He even had a flying ghoul that would moan as it swooped back and forth over the trick or treaters. It was going to be a banner year. So why did everything seem a little tawdry?

Because Dianne said he had some competition? "It's only Halloween decorations," he said to himself. But a cold lump filled Hank's stomach. *Maybe I'll take a walk after dinner,* he thought. *Check things out for myself.*

Nine o'clock found Hank on Beaumont

Street, a four pack of pumpkin ale in his hand. He recognized the house, a red brick two-story with a tiny front porch. It had a big yard. A rarity for homes this close to Pittsburgh, but the front lawn had always been choked with shrubs and brambles.

The new owner had manicured the dense growth into a fairy-land maze. Narrow paths lead off into tunnels of greenery. A pyramid of jack-o-lanterns blocked the central sidewalk leading to the front door. Trick or treaters would have to take one of the paths.

Hank stepped on to the nearest one. It was dark, and after a few feet, he felt claustrophobic. His head bumped into something hard hanging from a branch. "Dammit," he muttered. This wasn't scary, just dangerous.

"Hello." A voice came from the house. "Is someone there?"

Hank felt guilty, then angry at himself for the feeling. "Hey, sorry to bother you, I was just dropping by to say welcome to the neighborhood."

"Let me find the switch." The voice sounded friendly. "I'm the one who needs to apologize. I didn't make it easy to navigate out there."

Above Hank, A constellation of glass balls— blue, green, yellow—flickered into life. The light was gentle, not so much banishing the darkness as sculpting it, shaping the shadows into something beautiful. The flagstones making up the path were etched with complex patterns. Hank recognized a few shapes he'd seen on heavy metal t-shirts. The rest looked like bizarre geometry diagrams. Tiny jack-o-lanterns lined the paths edges.

It should have all been too pretty to be frightening, but Hank felt that tingly frisson at the base of his spine. It was the faces staring out at him from the foliage. They were placed perfectly, far enough away so at first you barely noticed. Then as you concentrated, the horrible

10

details came into focus. Hank reached past dark leaves to touch a hollow-eyed mask made of stiffened cloth. Below and to the left, a stone carving jutted out its rocky tongue in an obscene leer. There were more, each horrible in its own way.

"Over here."

Hank followed the voice. The twisting path finally lead back to the old central sidewalk. The glass balls hung like clusters of grapes all around him. More faces peered from the foliage. Hank felt overwhelmed with emotions, the foremost of which was jealousy. This was no cheap thrill. It was an experience.

A thin man in a tweed vest and matching pants stood on the porch smiling. He had close clipped blonde hair streaked with grey at the temples and wore round wire-rimmed glasses. He held a mug of tea in one large hand.

Hank swallowed his unkind feelings and attempted a smile of his own. "Wow, this is something." He stepped up on the porch and shook the hand extended to him.

"I'm Elliot Greer," the man said. His grip was firm. Cords of lean muscle stood out on his forearm. "So, you appreciate my little hobby?" He gestured at the display in the yard.

"Oh yeah," Hank said. "I do some Halloween decorating myself. My house is in the paper most years. Maybe you saw my place. It's over on Greenmount?"

"I'm afraid not. I've been so busy moving in and getting all this set up. I haven't had much time to get to know the neighborhood."

"Well, mine's a bit more gruesome. Bloody skulls, zombies. The kids love it. Yours seems almost Christmassy."

Greer stepped from the porch. He stroked the side of a blue globe filled with thin strands of stretched glass. "Actually, these are quite apropos of the season. They're called witch balls. The idea is that evil spirits become so fascinated by their beauty they trap themselves inside. A handy thing to have around Halloween."

Smartass, Hank thought. *Stop it. You barely know the guy.* "Witch balls huh? Still, a little pretty for my tastes. What I really like are the masks and sculptures. Creepy as hell."

Greer nodded.

"Where'd you get them anyway? I hit all the stores: Target, Walmart, Halloween World. You got a source online?"

"Africa."

"What?"

"Most, I acquired in Africa, some from South America and the Subcontinent. You can still find interesting pieces in the Mid-East, but a lot's been destroyed in the name of religion."

"Sure," said Hank, nodding. "I guess I won't look for them on eBay then, huh?"

"No, I suppose not," said Greer. "But, I'm probably boring you. Once I start going on about my collection..."

No, you're embarrassed for me, thought Hank. He stared down at his shoes and remembered the beer. *I should just take it home, but he probably saw it already.* "Hey, I brought over a welcome gift." Hank held up the four pack. "Pumpkin ale. It's good stuff."

Greer didn't reach for the gift. He gave Hank a pained smile. "It sounds intriguing, but I'm on a special diet. Rather hideous really, mostly leaves and sticks, I'm afraid." He held out the steaming china mug toward Hank. "Believe me, I'd prefer a good ale."

The stuff smelled rank. "Are those ashes floating in there?"

Greer looked sheepish. "Yes. It's burnt joss paper, an Asian thing. My diet is more folkway than medical prescription. When you collect the esoteric, you pick up a few odd beliefs along the way." He lifted the cup to his lips and sipped. "You wouldn't like it."

"I'll stick to beer," said Hank.

"Maybe, I could try one in the future?"

Hank took the words as a welcome chance to escape. "Sure. I better get going. More work to do on my place. Halloween is coming fast."

"I'm well aware," said Greer. "I look forward to seeing your... decorations."

Maybe he imagined it, but Hank thought he heard derision in those words. "Hey, before I go, I was wondering, aren't you a little worried?"

"What do you mean?"

"All those kids tramping through your yard, right down the middle of your *collection*. Things might get damaged."

Greer looked thoughtful. His eyes darted from one part of the yard to another. "I believe I have enough."

It was an odd response, Hank thought. "Some of the older kids like to do a little mayhem on purpose. I got four words for you: full-sized candy bars. None of those baby pretzel bags. You keep the little monsters happy, and you should be okay."

Greer nodded. "Thanks for the advice. Happy Halloween."

"Happy Halloween," said Hank. He walked out the way he'd come. No sooner had he stepped onto the street then Greer's yard went dark again. Hank could still see the witch balls and half hidden faces in his mind's eye. He had to admit Greer's collection was amazing, and that it pissed him off. *I don't get one thing that I can be the best at?* He popped the top on one of the pumpkin ales and took a long sip.

So, who's the bigger asshole, he wondered. *Greer for being so pompous, or me for being jealous.* He turned and walked home. Maybe he'd pick up an extra fog machine tomorrow.

Hank opened the Halloween edition of the *Collier Run Daily* and stared at a photo of Elliot Greer surrounded by glowing witch balls. "No big deal," Hank said to the empty kitchen.

"I've been in the paper plenty of times." It was Halloween, Hank's favorite day of the year and he was determined not to let Greer ruin it for him.

The weather that night was perfect, chilly but not cold, with enough breeze to blow the leaves around. Hank wore a vintage Pittsburgh Pirates uniform. He usually opted for something horrific, but last year Dianne had come over and sat with him on the porch. Hank figured she might have sat a good deal closer if his shirt hadn't been soaked in stage blood.

Jack-o-lanterns glowed from front porches up and down the street. Hank opened a pumpkin ale, switched on the fog machines, and waited for the monsters. At first, things went great. Ghosts and goblins traipsed up the steps, awestruck by Hank's handiwork. Parents oohed and ahhed like always, but this year there was a difference.

"Wow, you really outdid yourself, Hank"

"Thanks, it's a labor of love."

Then came the kicker. "Did you see that place over on Beaumont?"

Not everyone brought up Greer's amazing decorations. But enough did that Hank turned those mentions into his own sad little drinking game, taking a deep swig of beer every time Greer's collection' came up.

The second fog machine had been a bad idea. A thick mist covered the porch steps. A tiny Luke Skywalker slipped and cracked his shin on the cement. His mother—Princess Leia gone to seed—rushed up the stairs and helped the boy up. She glared at Hank, ignoring the chocolate bar in his hand.

"Your house is a menace," she hissed.

"Oh, come on, Luke there can't be more than two. You should be holding his hand." Hank regretted the words as soon as he said them. Too much beer, he thought.

"Screw you," Leia said. She picked up the

weeping Jedi and stalked down the street. Hank tried to turn off the fog machine but couldn't find the right cord in all the mist. He finally unplugged the whole power strip. The mist cleared, but when he turned the juice back on neither fog machine would work. Worse yet, the flying ghoul got tangled in its own wires and spent the rest of the night spinning in place, making a noise like a sick sheep. Hank didn't bother unplugging it.

He drank more and blamed Elliott Greer.

Dianne walked over around nine. She looked up at the bleating ghoul. "Are we experiencing some technical difficulties?"

"You could say that. It's not been the best evening."

"At least we have candy," Dianne held out a handful of fun size snickers.

Maybe the night doesn't have to end bad, Hank thought. He made room for her on the porch step. An empty beer bottle wobbled beside him. He tried to steady it but misjudged the distance and sent it tumbling down the steps. The bottle shattered with a crash. Hank's lunge almost sent him tumbling after it, but Dianne caught his arm.

"Goddammit, this just isn't my night."

Dianne looked at the collection of empty bottles. "Maybe we should have a little coffee with our candy."

"Or *maybe,* I can drink what I want to on my own porch."

Dianne's warm smile froze.

"Oh Jesus, Di, I'm sorry. It's just the fog machines broke down, and that stupid flying ghoul got hung up. The damned thing cost me a hundred bucks."

"So, you got drunk because your toys didn't work. Makes sense."

"Dianne, really. I apologize. I'll make that coffee."

"No. Your porch your rules. Have another

beer, I'm going home."

"Come on, don't be like that."

Dianne walked down the stairs stepping carefully over the broken glass. "Happy Halloween, Hank."

Hank watched her go. She was right. He was acting like a baby. "I think I'll get that coffee." He stood up and walked to the door. As he turned the knob, laughter rent the night, and an egg burst against the wall inches from his head.

Hank flung himself inside and pulled his home-security baseball bat out of the umbrella stand. He rushed back on to the porch, scanning the streets for attackers. A block away, dark laughing shapes disappeared between two houses.

Hank shook his head. What the hell was he going to do, send some teenager to the hospital for throwing an egg? Besides, there'd been at least four shapes, and they hadn't looked small. Like he'd told Greer, the bigger kids could get up to some real mayhem on Halloween. Hank let that thought linger for a minute.

Maybe one more beer after all, and a walk. Probably should take the bat along. Never can tell what you might run into.

Beaumont Street was dark. It was after eleven, and most folks had blown out their pumpkins and gone to bed. Only the Greer residence still glowed with the light of witch balls and jack-o-lanterns.

I wouldn't have bought that second fog machine if it hadn't been for Greer. Wouldn't have drank so much either. I'd be sitting with Dianne right now. Hank knew it was all bullshit, but alcohol and jealousy were more than a match for his common sense.

He looked up and down the street. He'd changed into dark sweats, hoping to look like just another teenager to anyone gazing out their window. He held the bat close to his leg and stepped onto the nearest path. Even through

13

his drunken anger he still couldn't deny Greer's collection was amazing. The realization only pissed him off more.

He brought the bat up to his shoulder and swung. If he'd had a plan at all, it had been to smash a couple of the, no doubt expensive, witch balls and run. Go home and let the thought of Greer sweeping up bits of his precious collection tomorrow lull him to sleep. Something changed as Hank shattered his first target. Colored glass rained down, and Hank's heart filled with a fierce joy.

"Pretentious little shit," he grunted, as he swung the bat in short, vicious arcs. He wasn't running away. The plan was forgotten. Hank pushed forward, stomping jack-o-lanterns to orange pulp, kicking over sculptures Greer had *acquired* on the god-damned subcontinent. It wasn't about the decorations anymore. It was about the divorce—his wife living with that banker in Harrisburg. It was about being two months late on the mortgage, it was every failure and indignity Hank had ever suffered in a life full of them. He knew it wasn't Greer's fault and didn't care. He had a target now, and couldn't stop if he wanted to.

Someone shouted. Arms like cables locked themselves around Hank's neck. He tried to swing the bat, but his arms didn't want to work anymore. Hank felt himself lifted and thrown. He landed hard on wood. Blood rushed to his brain. The first thing he saw was Elliot Greer, his back turned, staring up at a blue-green ball of glass. Hank didn't see any others. *Did I smash them all? Jesus.*

The second thing Hank noticed was the pistol in Greer's hand.

His face red with rage, Greer turned. He didn't raise the gun. "Who sent you?"

Hank stared up at the man. He didn't understand the question and feared whatever he said would be wrong.

"Xiǎnshì zìjì, datgelu eich hunan, Aratǎte?" Greer moved closer, shouting more indecipherable questions at Hank with each step.

"Please, I don't understand," Hank said. "I'm sorry, just don't shoot."

Greer looked down at the gun, seeming almost surprised to see it there. "Who are you?" he asked.

"What?" Fear still burned bright, but another emotion mixed with it. Hank was insulted. "Hank Swafford, I live on Greenmount, I came over with beer."

"Hank? The Halloween-decoration guy."

There it was again—*decoration.* "Why do you have to say it that way. It's my thing. I'm good at it. I used to be the best, at least around here." Anger gave Hank the strength to sit up. He still held the bat. "Then you showed up with your masks and goddamned witch balls." He used the bat as a crutch and was almost upright when Greer gave him a vicious kick in the ribs. Hank toppled, gasping for breath.

Another kick sent the bat into the yard. Greer stood over Hank, and now the gun was most definitely being aimed. "You destroyed my defenses because I upstaged your paper-mâché tombstones. What is wrong with you?"

The black hole of the gun barrel filled Hank's vision. "Jesus, I'll pay for it all. Have me arrested. I deserve it."

"Stand up." Greer looked down at his wristwatch then out into the yard. "I said, stand up."

"No. Call the police. I'll just wait here." The last of Hank's beer-fueled haze had burned away. Greer was going to kill him. "This doesn't have to get any worse."

Greer rubbed a hand across his face. "Oh, I'm afraid it does. Now, stand up."

Hank didn't move.

"I'm not going to kill you, but I will wound

14

you in some very nasty places if you don't stand up right now."

Hank stood.

Greer gestured to a rocking chair on the porch. "Sit down. There's a cup of tea on the table beside you. Drink it."

Hank lifted the cup. He recognized the foul smell from the first time he'd been here. "What's in it?"

"Burnt paper, remember? Some herbs. It gives perspective. Now, drink it, or I'll put a bullet in your crotch."

Hank put the cup to his lips and drank. It tasted better than it smelled, like smoked wine.

"That wasn't so bad, was it? Finish up."

Hank lifted the cup and drained it. He looked past Greer to the one remaining witch ball. The light it gave off took substance. Glowing geometric shapes spread out from the ball in all directions—spheres within cubes, joining and releasing to form new and more complex patterns. "You drugged me," Hank said.

"No, just a little Taoist magic. Gives you yin-yang eyes. Let's you see what others can't."

There was no darkness. Hank saw the world with a clarity that came close to overwhelming him—the grain of the boards that made up the porch, the soft inner glow of the atomic processes that held it all together. "I can see... everything."

"Yes, it's not something you'll thank me for. Now listen to me. You have no idea what you've done, so I'm going to tell you. I'm a thief Hank, but not some simple smash and grab man. I started with tombs, and I learned things. I learned you can steal secrets more valuable than gold."

"What's that noise?" Hank asked. It was far away but distinctive—the electric whine of cicadas as interpreted by a children's choir.

"Ignore it."

"Something's coming." Hank stood despite the gun. He couldn't help himself. This must be the way prey felt when the big carnivores showed up. He had to get out of there. The side of the pistol whipped against Hank's jaw. Greer pushed him back on to the rocker.

"Don't worry, we have a little time yet."

Hank wiped blood from the corner of his mouth. He didn't try to stand again.

"I was a very successful thief," Greer said. "I plundered temples, even robbed a god or two."

"You're crazy." But Hank's voice lacked conviction. His ears buzzed with the whine of cicadas.

"Made some enemies along the way, as you'd expect. A bad lot. But I had my secrets. Knew how to stay a few steps ahead. Keep moving, that's the key. Boats are good. They don't like running water. Flying's even better. There are rules to the game though, and one night a year I have to sit tight on solid ground. Do you see where I'm going with this, Hank? Can you guess what that night is? Here's a hint, it's a time of year when you like to decorate, and it's not Christmas."

"Halloween?"

"I knew you could do it." Greer was shouting now, the gun pointed up at the night sky. Hank lunged past the man toward the sidewalk. Greer laughed. He kicked the back of Hank's knee sending him sprawling. Hank tried to crawl. Glass from shattered witch balls gouged his hands and knees. A foot slammed into his crotch from behind, and he fell to his belly and retched.

"Just a few more words, Hank." Greer squatted and lifted Hank's chin until they were gazing eye to eye. "So, how do I keep my enemies at bay on that one night? Not guns, Hank. Bullets wouldn't phase them a bit, I'm afraid. But I had my defenses. I was always ready, and this year was no exception. I rented a new place in middle-of-nowhere Pennsylvania. There's a creek behind the house. Like I said, they don't like running water. I put up my defenses in front, a maze of distractions, wards, and traps. The only thing I didn't account for was you."

Greer shook his head. "You and your pathetic decorations. The good news is I can still get away. It's going to be tricky. I'll need your help. I think that you owe me at least that much."

"What do want me to do?"

"Only to be here. I have to stay a little longer. Let them feel my presence. Thanks to you, I'm forced to leave everything behind. No baggage. It's the only way I'll stay ahead of them. Even traveling light, they'd still catch me. That's where you come in, Hank. You're my diversion. Someone they can take their anger out on when they discover I'm gone. The time it takes them to rip your soul apart will be my head start. I think you'll agree that's fair."

Greer cocked the pistol. He looked at his watch, then sniffed the air. The wind bore the smell of ozone mixed with raw sewage. "It's time," said Greer. "Look at me. You said you liked things on the gory side."

Greer shoved the barrel of the gun beneath his own chin and pulled the trigger. The report was muffled, but the results were spectacular. A geyser of blood, bone, and brain erupted from the top of Greer's skull. But Hank had yin-yang eyes now, and he saw more. Amidst the viscera rose a living light, the soul of Elliot Greer. It circled the remaining witch ball twice and then shot upward through the trees.

Greer's corpse—the baggage he had to leave behind—toppled to the ground.

Now the things hunting the man would come and take their disappointment out on Hank. He could hear the creatures advance, smell their stench on the wind.

Hank rushed to the front door. He wouldn't be anyone's diversion. Greer had said the creek behind the house offered some protection. He would go there. The door was locked. Hank slammed his shoulder into the thick wood, but it didn't budge.

An icy chill struck Hank like a blow. The electric cicada whine rose into a howling storm. Hank turned as something dark rushed up the pathway toward him. The yin-yang eyes had revealed the inner light that filled all things. The creature approaching had no light. It was a void clawing its way through reality to reach the enemy it sought. Hank pressed himself against the door. He was going to die. No, it would be worse than that. His stupidity had brought Hank to the notice of creatures who considered death only the opening act.

The thing stopped. Hank didn't dare move. Didn't breathe. The void scudded toward the last glowing witch ball, weaving through the complex geometry of light the ball gave off. The creature circled the witch ball once, twice, then flowed inside it. There was a whistling sound. The sphere glowed white then faded to a dull black.

The goddamn balls work, Hank thought and cursed himself for taking a bat to them. There was time now. He'd circle the house to the creek. He made it three steps before they found him. Creatures filled the yard. More of the clawing voids, but other things as well. A cloud of metallic white butterflies, each wing edge a razor that rang against its neighbor, filled the air with the sound of bells. A giant man, naked and grotesquely obese dragged himself forward. Cloven hooved children hung from his mountain of flesh, tearing away bloody mouthfuls and smacking their lips.

"Greer's dead," Hank yelled. The things in

16

the yard didn't care. Elliot Greer would get his head start. As the creatures descended on him, Hank had to admit it was a really scary effect.

Frank Oreto is a writer and editor of weird fiction living in Pittsburgh, Pennsylvania. When not penning strange tales of the supernatural, he can be found cooking elaborate meals for his wife and three voracious children.

Everything Gothic

by Carl Hughes

WALLACE GUMMER IS pissed off. Driving through the bleak winter countryside he knows he's had a wasted day: a pointless trip to a distant town on an abortive errand to secure more gothic items for his collection. The advert in the local paper had promised gothic antiques galore, but on Wallace's arrival at the shop he'd found only imperfect plaster casts and trivial trinkets. The shop owner, a wizened creature with bulbous eyes like a frog, had tried to sell him a plaster skull with the assurance that it came from the corpse of Abraham Lincoln and was the genuine article.

The moorland on either side of the road stretches for miles in the brooding gloom of a December afternoon. A few hardy hikers in blue and purple hats are striding out, but otherwise the vista could have come from Cambrian times. The only other traffic consists of the occasional car, some with tinsel wound around the antennas. Wallace isn't in a tinsel mood.

Over a rise he comes to a straight stretch of

18

road, beside which stands what could be a Victorian rectory with gables and turrets. He frowns. He could have sworn the place wasn't there yesterday. Ridiculous, of course. Slowing, he sees a sign outside reading Everything Gothic—Art Gallery. There's a tiny parking lot at the side, and Wallace pulls into it. As an art aficionado, with a special interest in the gothic, he can't resist the lure to take a look inside.

Clammy dampness envelopes him as soon as he leaves the car. It's as if the day is threaded with veins of glacial death that laugh in the face of a distant spring. Wasting no time, he hurries to the front of the building. A sign over the door says Enos Garns, Proprietor.

Inside, he's greeted by the smell of polish and old canvas, of oil paints and ancient dust. There's also a fuggy warmth, cosseting after the chill outside.

Wallace is startled when a figure looms out of the shadows. It's a gaunt, cadaverous individual with yellow teeth and piercing black eyes. The man could have been an undertaker spawned from the pen of Dickens. "Can I be of assistance?" he inquires.

"Are you Mr Garns?" Wallace asks.

"At your service." The man gives a little bow—also Dickensian.

Wallace gazes around. The walls are hung with pictures of varying sizes; some in oils, some in watercolors, a few in charcoal. He inhales again. The odors please him. He says, "There can't be much business in such an isolated spot. Surely an art gallery needs to be in the centre of town."

Garns cocks his head. With a predatory smile, he says, "This place is only for the discerning, sir, not the mere curious."

Wallace interprets that smile as an indication that Garns thinks he's found a dupe who'll be fooled with any old junk. Well, you've picked the wrong one here, Mr Garns, he thinks. "May I look around?" he asks.

"But of course. Please take your time and if you have any questions don't hesitate to ask."

Wallace moves among the displays. To his disappointment he finds the works, without exception, to be dull, flat and utterly uninspiring. He says as much to Enos Garns, who's been trailing behind at a not-too-discreet distance.

"Take this one, for instance," Wallace says, stopping in front of an oil painting of a neglected graveyard with a derelict church in the background, all seen by cold wintry moonlight. "It looks as if it's been created by an amateur using painting-by-numbers."

"Actually, sir, that painting is a work of genius, but it's necessary to view it through a special pair of spectacles in order to appreciate its subtleties," Garns says.

Wallace laughs scornfully, but Garns produces, as if by sleight of hand, a set of black-rimmed glasses. He invites his visitor to put them on.

Sceptical, Wallace humors the man by slipping on the glasses. Instantly the picture appears in the most incredible and atmospheric detail; every gothic nuance accentuated and perfect in its structure and expression. Electrified, Wallace finds his pulse racing like some wild beast let loose from a zoo. He must have this picture at any cost. It's unlike anything he's ever conceived of owning. Its detail is absolutely unique in its brooding intensity. Concealing his excitement, however, he remarks indifferently, "I might be interested in acquiring the piece for my collection, provided the price is reasonable."

Garns grins his yellow-toothed smile and names a price far below what Wallace had been prepared to pay. The cadaverous man waits, still smiling, his eyes as glowing as embers on a Christmas fire.

"Very well, but I must have the glasses too," Wallace says. "Otherwise visitors to my home will think I'm a fool for buying such an insipid thing."

"Naturally, sir, the spectacles come as part of the package," Garns assures him.

Ten minutes later Wallace is in his car with the picture wrapped in brown paper and secured with string. He's feeling exultant. This has been a superb day after all. His acquisition will take pride of place among all the gothic items in his collection.

Twilight is drawing in on the short winter afternoon as he re-emerges on to the moorland road. Within an hour he's home: a flat in an immaculate building, with a concierge guarding the lobby, and silent elevators to all floors. Wallace lives on the third floor, his lounge window overlooking the municipal cemetery, where on moonlit nights it's possible to imagine white-shrouded wraiths flitting between the tombstones.

After shedding his coat he unwraps the prized painting and hangs it in pride of place on his bedroom wall. There, he'll be able to relish it to his heart's desire immediately before descending into a gothic-filled dream, and will see it again as soon as he awakens.

That evening he spends an hour gazing at the picture, absorbing its essence into his soul, and falls asleep still wearing the special glasses.

He's awoken by the hooting of an owl, so nearby he's instantly catapulted into full consciousness. At first his senses are scrambled. What he sees can't be true. He's no longer in bed, but in the derelict graveyard of his picture. He is wearing the gear he always dons for exploring old churchyards and cemeteries. There's a marrow-deep chill that has him shuddering, but he realizes the trembling isn't caused only by the frosty air. He's panic-stricken. How did he get here?

He stares around, his gaze flicking from the church, lit by baleful moonlight, to the slanting tombstones with their green-and-yellow lichen. His breath is pluming in gasping vapor. Then he hears movement: a furtive, slithery sound coming from behind a tombstone. An intense sense of dread and menace descend on him like a funeral mantle and he realises at some primal level that he's in mortal danger. This isn't one of his dreams. This is far more real than anything he's ever experienced.

Terrified, without conscious thought of action or repercussions, he bolts between the graves, his feet catching in the undergrowth and sending up little plumes of frost like malign fairy dust. Lead seems to be dragging at his feet, or it's as if he's struggling through a mire. At last, with his lungs almost bursting, he reaches the lichgate and scrambles out on to the lane beyond. At once he realizes there's no safety there. He's being stalked—pursued by something nameless and obscene. Racing down the narrow lane which is bordered by stark, naked trees with branches like ancient bones, he remembers that extract from *The Rime Of The Ancient Mariner* by Samuel Taylor Coleridge: *Like one who on a lonely road doth walk in fear and dread, and having once turned round, walks on and turns no more his head; because he knows a frightful fiend doth close behind him tread.*

His feet pound the frost-hardened surface of the lane. Though once muddy, it is now frozen into ridges and spikes that threaten to unhinge his ankles. At least he's no longer treading through a mire. He's sprinting faster than any time since his schooldays. He can hear something—something—pursuing him and probably gaining ground. He lets loose a terrified shriek.

Then, round a bend, he comes to Enos Garns's gallery standing half concealed in woodland, in a place it has no business being. No matter—it might offer sanctuary. Exerting himself until he fears his heart will burst, he flings open the door and tumbles inside the place. He's beside himself with panic and horror. He knows in another

20

few seconds the fiend, or demon, or whatever was in his wake, would have been upon him.

He finds he's grovelling at the feet of Enos Garns, the proprietor of Everything Gothic. The man is looking down at him with gaunt equanimity.

Grabbing the hem of Garns's trousers as if they're a lifeline to a different and more mortal world, Wallace cries, "Save me from whatever you've let loose from that painting!"

"Of course, my friend," Garns soothes. "Just hand me back those magic spectacles."

Until now, Wallace hasn't even realized he's still wearing them. He wrenches them off and flings them into Garns outstretched palm.

Suddenly there's a great crash of thunder, a rolling of reality, as if an immense earthquake has erupted from the planet's core. Wallace finds himself back in the graveyard. He cries out, but it's little more than a bleat of animal terror. He knows the fiend is now closer than ever and he stares around in dread.

In the same second, everything seems to shrink and draw away, as if vanishing into a distant chasm, taking him with it. Worse, he finds he's paralysed. The mask of terror on his face is fastened there in perpetual and lavish detail.

Even as that realization strikes him, it's as if he's looking out into Enos Garns gallery. Garns is showing a sporty looking young man the picture.

"It's dull, flat and uninspiring," the man is saying. "It looks as if it's been created by an amateur using painting-by-numbers."

Garns assures the patron that the picture is a work of genius, but in order to appreciate its nuances, it must be viewed through a special pair of glasses.

Which he then produces.

Carl Hughes is a freelance journalist and writer. He is married to Linda, and they live in Norfolk, a county in the East Anglia region of England. He has worked for the national and provincial press in the UK, and is an award winning writer. His stories and articles have appeared in numerous magazines and literary journals. Carl writes all kinds of fiction, but has a special love for horror.

21

Her Face

By Dennis Warren

Illustration by Kira Sokolovskaia. Image first published in the anthology, *Cat O' Nine Tales*.

THERE WAS NO doubt about it. I was lost. This was supposed to be a shortcut! A review of my map prior to embarking upon the journey seemed to indicate this route to be the shortest distance for the trip. I was certain, at the time, that this particular path would take me to the location of my latest job interview in the least amount of time. My plan was to arrive early, and therefore make a good impression. However, it was now hours beyond the appointed time. Most certainly, my absence from the meeting did not produce the desired effect.

In retrospect, I realize I must have taken a wrong turn somewhere. Or was it just fate? In light of the events which transpired on that road, I am not convinced this was an error, or bad luck. There are forces beyond our comprehension which guide and direct us in this life, whether we believe them to affect us or not. Of this, I am now certain.

I was miles away from any recognizable landmark on the map, but continued to navigate my way throughout the winding country road. The pavement had long ago turned to gravel and dirt. I made many right and left turns down ever narrowing avenues. So at this point, I did not have confidence that I would be able to retrace my path in reverse. Being in such a remote location, there was no option to stop and ask for directions. Reluctantly, I resolved myself to continue forward until I had the chance to do so.

I kept my hopes up as I drove onward through the wilderness. Certainly at some point I would emerge from this shadowy forest. I envisioned the moment when I would elude the thickening wood to exit triumphantly onto an Interstate. Oh the joy! The gas gauge was about to dip into the red. I needed to refuel myself, too. It had been a long time since I could refresh with a sip of cola, or a bite of some Little Debbie snack cake. My stomach began to rumble. A truck stop or even a lonesome country store would seem a form of eternal salvation to me. I would celebrate my victory at the very first glimpse of civilization.

However, at the moment, the trees became larger and denser. A web of branches loomed above me as I drove through the narrow roadway. There did not appear to be an end in sight. The overhang of greenery above the road blotted out the sun. Strangely, a sense of odd claustrophobia began to grip me. I became nervous, uneasy. Would I ever make it out of this accursed timber alive? My mind wandered as I convinced myself that there would soon be someone to assist me. Yes, someone would appear to lead this weary, disturbed soul back on course.

Then I saw her. It was a lady dressed in a long, flowing gown…walking through the forest! She had just appeared from behind a large tree. The light was getting dim, but there was no mistaking what I had seen. I slowed the vehicle to a crawl to get a better look. But there was nothing there. I was tired, and suggested to myself that perhaps, due to fatigue, I could be experiencing some mild form of hallucination. But then, I blinked…and there she was again! Strolling gracefully through the thicket, the elegant lady made her way through the woods just a short distance from the road.

I applied the brakes and came to an abrupt halt. I rolled down my window and called out to her repeatedly. During her slow, steady stride through the heavy maze of wood, she made no gesture or acknowledgement of any kind. I honked the horn, loudly, several times. No response. Either I was being blatantly ignored, or this person was most assuredly deaf. I pulled up my parking brake. Then I left the vehicle running and exited it to begin making my way toward the lady. As I entered the dense forest, I called again at the top of my lungs. She stopped and turned!

The light was fading fast. Although I could not quite make out her full form, I sensed her gaze to be one of a most sullen expression. I wondered who she was and how she came to be wandering all alone in such a foreboding wilderness. After a brief exchange of glances, she turned away, and began to walk deeper into the woods. I shouted to her again, and she again looked back at me. I was still unable to make out her features completely. She beckoned me to follow, and once again turned to resume her steady pace into the labyrinth of trees.

I looked back to the road, marking the location of my vehicle, and careful to keep a watchful eye on the still running car. My strategy was to use the streaming headlights as a guide for returning. I was determined to convince this woman to accompany me back to civilization. I reasoned that we would be able to make our way back toward these beams once I had caught up to her. Most assuredly she was a local, and therefore would be able to supply the directions which could lead to our freedom from this green hell of seclusion. I was sure she would not refuse some transportation to her home or another location in return for simple directions out of here.

As I followed her into those woods, my mind raced in an attempt to make sense of what was happening. Who is this woman, really? Was it possible her home was just steps away? Maybe I could make a phone call, or access a new map to gain my bearings? No, this was strange. The truth was bleak. Here I was, traipsing into the blackening forest; pursuing some unknown female I had not even formally met. What is her name? Why in the world is she walking leisurely through these woods, hours away from humanity of any kind?

A light fog began to descend. Visibility became even more blurred. I turned around to see if I could still find my way back to the vehicle. There was but a tiny glow in the distance. The car seemed to be miles away. I knew this was not the case. No, it was just an illusion created by the fog. I steeled myself and resumed following this enigma that appeared to be a woman. She was farther away now, as I had lingered for awhile wondering if I should turn back. The lady seemed to sense my anxiety and stopped. She extended her arm toward me, and beckoned me forward with a delicate hand. I was mesmerized by her vague loveliness. At the same time, I was also terrified of becoming even more lost than I already was. Where could she possibly be leading me?

Once again, I followed her. The fog grew thicker. In between a mass of trees the graceful lady seemed to disappear. Then in the distance, from behind another grouping of trees she would once again reappear. The eeriness of this predicament began to dawn on me. I shivered in the twilight. Was it truly getting cooler, or was it something else? So cold all of a sudden, it seemed. Regardless of the reason, I felt as if I was freezing, and the knowledge that complete darkness would soon be upon us did not comfort me.

My vehicle was nowhere in sight now. I then knew I was in very great danger of becoming completely disoriented. Was I already lost? How long had it been since I entered the forest on foot? Once more, I entertained thoughts of turning back, and lingered. Hesitatingly, I looked back in her direction again. This time, somehow…through the fog, and all the tangled mess, our eyes met. So warm! So inviting! Her gaze enthralled me, and rejuvenated my spirit! All hope returned with but a brief glimpse of her beautiful face. Then at once she turned away, and continued her quest, moving further into the woods. The time to solve this mystery

was now or never!

I sped my pace and felt branches scraping at my chest. Limbs slapped my lips and brow. I tripped over a fallen tree and bit the dirt hard. A bit dazed, but uninjured, I picked myself up and raced toward the lady with all the speed I could muster. The deeper we ventured, the darker it became, but I was only a few steps away from her now. I called out to her again, and again, but she did not answer me. Suddenly, she turned and vanished behind a large tree. I dashed after her with recklessness, snapping branches, and half tripping myself in the process. But I was stopped dead in my tracks at the sight that lay before me.

Sweat dripping down my neck, I gasped in horror…choked back the urge to scream. For right in front of me on the forest floor rested the decaying skeletal remains of someone dressed in a long, white evening gown. It was evident this person had been lying there a long while. Dead leaves, tangled roots, and discarded tree branches covered most of the once living corpse. This was the pitiful grave of someone who had met their demise deep within this damned forest. I wondered where my lady friend had gone…but then slowly, like a slow-motion locomotive, it hit me. Finally, I understood. And I shuddered. I stared into those dark sockets of the wretched skull and realized just who it was I was staring at. Then those blackened holes which once contained eyes stared back at me.

She showed me her face, her true face… one more time. Her face…a face of immense beauty! Shining in glory! A bright face filled with compassion and love. Eyes of fire! Smile gleaming with the radiance of the sun! Her visage was so appealing it would certainly have been the reason that the angels sing with joy and the very gods themselves descended from the heavens above. The type of beauty an immortal would risk their soul for. Just to enjoy the company of such exquisite fairness. But then, as quickly as the apparition manifested, it was gone. Once again I found myself staring into a cold, dead, eyeless skull.

I screamed. With every ounce of fury and power I had left within my being, and at the top of my lungs, I screamed! Then I sprinted back in the direction of my car. The fog had lifted, and I could see a glow. There it was! Still running, parked on the road where I had left it. I would guess that I must have wandered aimlessly in the forest for at least a half an hour. But I swear, with blazing speed, I returned to my car in seconds. I put the machine in gear and pressed the pedal to the floor. Dust and gravel were kicked into the air as I sped down the tiny road. Within minutes, to my great surprise and relief, I found myself once more driving upon solid pavement. Soon afterward I spied an exit sign. This led to an Interstate, and eventually my victorious arrival at a gas station to refuel and gorge myself upon a bounty of junk food.

I returned home. The following day I reported the incident to the local police. They were very interested in my story, and encouraged me to assist them in a search. During the brightest part of the daylight, of course, I joined them and helped identify the location. I was able to lead them directly to the spot where the dreadful remains of a once beauteous woman lay decaying. The authorities questioned me for several hours about my involvement. I'm sure it was their duty to immediately suspect me as being part of a heinous murder. However, it was soon revealed to them through research and investigation that the remains were those of a woman who had gone missing many years ago. It seems she had been abducted and murdered by a lecherous man with a history of despicable crimes toward women. The culprit had long ago met his own brutal demise at the hands of an angry mob. It was quite a sensational story. The police then released me, and indeed thanked me for my strange assistance in solving the mystery, as there was no reason to suspect my involvement in the crime.

As unbelievable as it may sound, every aspect of my story is absolutely true. I would encourage each of you to ponder long and hard about the consequences of taking shortcuts in your lives. Take my experience as a warning. For the seemingly shortest route is not always the best path to take. However, I for one am very grateful for the uncanny adventure I have just shared. It is the only time in my life which I can say for certain that I have definitely encountered what might be called "the supernatural". And I have never again beheld such beauty from anyone among the living. No, I will never forget that evening, in the middle of a lonely, dark forest. That single moment in time when I stared into her face and she stared back at me. It is burned into my very being. I replay it often in my mind, to make me smile. To give me hope, to bring me peace. That moment when a lady of true elegance and grace…though deceased, showed me her face.

Dennis Warren is a man of diverse talents. He has performed as vocalist and drummer for several Virginia based heavy metal bands including Play War, Cryptameria, and Cult of Dionysis. He is a comic book creator and artist, who has released several issues of the heavy metal science fiction comic book series Metalcult Comix, and the children's comic/coloring book series Flippy The Dachshund.

Dennis performs as the professional wrestling personality, The Spectacular Stache. When he's not playing music, creating comics, or wrestling, he likes to write scary ghost stories and weird tales of the supernatural.

25

The Invitation

by Ken Kreps

JACK CRANDALL WAS not an easy man to like. In fact, he was impossible to like. He used people with only one thought in mind: how would they benefit the wellbeing, comfort and advancement of Jack Crandall. He was powerful, crafty and smart, and nothing stood in his way. As we join Jack, he sits at his huge mahogany desk during the middle of the business day.

"Sandi, get in here."

"Yes, Mr. Crandall."

"Look at this. Just look at this."

"Ahh, I'm…I'm sorry, sir. I…I don't understand," Sandi stammered.

"You don't understand? I asked you to do one simple task. I told you to put these reports in three-ring binders, not spiral binders. Do you want me to look like a fool when I present this to the board? Is that what you want?"

"No…no, sir. I…I was sure you said spiral."

Jack exhaled a long-suffering sigh. "Tell me Sandi, do you like working here?"

"Yes, sir, I do."

"Well, one more gaffe like this and you won't be. Is that clear?"

"Yes, sir."

"Then bind them correctly and have them

on my desk by eight o'clock Monday morning."

"But, Mr. Crandall, the board meeting isn't for two weeks. You know I have evening classes at the university this week. I'll have to work over the weekend to have the new reports to you by Monday."

"I don't care. Just do it. Is that understood?"

Sandi nodded meekly before scurrying out of the office.

"*Someday I have got to get rid of her. She's worthless*," Jack thought.

Without warning the door to his office opened again.

"Now what?" Jack asked. He was obviously irritated.

"Sorry, Mr. Crandall…I forgot," Sandi said, "This came for you about fifteen minutes ago." She placed a plain white envelope on his desk and hurriedly left the office.

Jack picked it up and turned it over in his hands. *I wonder what this is*, he thought. *Expensive envelope….no stamp or return address. Hmmm.*

He opened the envelope to find a beautifully engraved note.

It read:

> *Dear Mr. Crandall,*
> *You are cordially invited to a formal dinner tomorrow at eight PM. You'll enjoy a dining affair unlike any you've ever experienced in the past. This event is only for those with the most discriminating taste. Please RSVP to 555-1387.*

"Sandi, get in here," he shouted.

"Yes, sir?"

"Is this some kind of joke?"

"I beg your pardon?"

"This letter—where did it come from?"

Sandi shrugged. "I don't really know, sir."

"You don't know?"

"It was on my desk when I came back from the lady's room."

"Did you see who left it?"

"No, sir."

"It was just sitting there when you returned?"

"Yes sir, right in the middle of my desk."

He looked at her sternly before saying, "All right. Get back to work."

I don't have time for this, he thought.

He read the note a second time. A dining affair unlike any I've ever experienced in the past. *Yeah, I'll bet. Still, I do have discriminating taste. Maybe I'll call them. What could it hurt?*

He dialed the number on the note. After a few rings a man answered. "Hello."

"Yes, hello. This is Jack Crandall and I…"

"Ah, yes, Mr. Crandall, we've been expecting your call."

"Well, you shouldn't have, pal. I'm not even sure why I'm calling."

"Why, I assume it is to accept our invitation."

"Now, just a minute. I didn't say anything about accepting. You have to admit, your invitation didn't give much detail."

"We keep a very low profile, Mr. Crandall. Very few people know about us."

"Us? Exactly who is *us*?"

"The West Side Dining Club."

"Oh, you're some kind of new restaurant," Jack said.

"No, not at all. We're a private club— not open to the public. We only serve by invitation."

"I see. Why the west side? That's not exactly the best part of town."

"This location works well for us. I think you'll find our accommodations to be quite luxurious."

"I know this town pretty well. How come I've never heard of you?"

"As I said, sir, we're not widely known, and only serve dinner by invitation."

"And just who are you?"

"My name is Mr. Maricopa. I am the president of the West Side Dining Club."

"And how did you come to invite me to your club?"

"We have quite rigid standards, Mr. Crandall.

27

Let's just say you fit the criteria we look for. It's really that simple."

"Criteria? What criteria?"

"Oh, accomplishments, items like that," Maricopa offered vaguely.

"You've probably heard about my business career," Jack boasted.

"Oh, yes, sir, indeed we have."

"So…ahh…you have these dinners once a week…once a month, what?"

"Actually, Mr. Crandall, we host only one dinner per year."

"Once a year?" Jack said sounding surprised.

"Yes. As I said, we're quite exclusive. We host one dinner annually and invite one new guest of honor each year."

Jack was liking this more and more. "So, this year you're honoring me?"

"Yes indeed, and might I say, we're looking forward to serving you."

Jack was still suspicious. "Okay, pal, how much is this exclusive dinner going to cost me?"

"Oh, there's no charge, Mr. Crandall. You'll be our guest."

"Well…. I…"

"The dinner is entirely complimentary, as is the champagne."

"Champagne, you say?"

"Quite a rare vintage. If you could buy it, you would pay somewhere in the neighborhood of twelve hundred dollars per bottle."

Jack chuckled. "That's a pretty nice neighborhood."

"Oh, I'm sure you'll find it quite satisfactory."

"Tomorrow evening is awfully short notice."

"Will that be a problem?"

"No, I can shift a few things around. I'll attend your little dinner party. I need to know where you're located."

"That won't be necessary. We'll send a car for you."

"Really?"

"Yes. Our limousine will pick you up at your house at seven PM."

"A limo, expensive champagne, you guys go all out don't you?"

"As I said, sir, it's our pleasure to serve you."

"Okay, I'll be ready at seven. Formal attire?"

"Yes, please. Oh, and there is one more item to discuss."

"Yeah?"

"We only have one rule, but it's quite firm."

"I'm listening."

"As I mentioned, we keep an extremely low profile. It helps keep the riff-raff out. I'm sure you understand"

"Sure."

"Therefore, you must tell no one about this honor. If you do, your invitation will be withdrawn."

"I understand."

"Good bye, sir. We'll look forward to seeing you tomorrow."

As Jack hung up the phone he smiled and thought, *Chosen for my accomplishments, am I? Well, maybe these guys are okay after all.*

〰〰〰

The next morning, flush with anticipation for the evening ahead, Jack sat at his desk. He was thinking about a big and lucrative project his company was working on.

"Ted, get in here," he shouted to one of his three assistants down the hall.

"Sir?" Ted asked as he entered the office.

"Close the door," Jack commanded. "What's the latest on the Jacksboro acquisition?"

Ted lowered his head and shuffled his feet. "Well, I'm afraid it's not going very well."

"What do you mean, not going well?" Jack snapped.

"Well, sir, the tenants in one of the buildings are refusing to sell their condos. In fact, they've hired an attorney to block the entire sale."

"Can't we buy them off?"

"Ah, they're a stubborn group. They say their building is simply not for sale. They won't budge."

"What the hell?" Jack fumed. "Get the damn building condemned, Ted. We can pay off the city inspectors to condemn it, and then reverse it after we own the property."

"Sir, that building is in A-1 condition. I don't see how…"

"We have city inspectors who'll do anything for money. Offer them enough and they'll do it."

"Mr. Crandall, many of the people in that building are quite elderly, and some are not well."

"Oh, please. They are all loaded or they couldn't live in a building that ritzy. It would be a minor inconvenience for them."

Ted shook his head. "It would be much more than a minor inconvenience. Some of the people we are trying to force to sell have lived there for over twenty years. Moving would be a great hardship for many of them and…"

"Do you think I care about a bunch of rich old farts hardships? Whatever their problems might be, that's too damned bad. I have a business to run, and that building is a gold mine."

"But, sir…" Ted protested.

"What's with this bleeding-heart crap? Life is tough, mister. The strong survive and the weak don't. That's just the way it is. You'd better learn that, and you'd better learn it fast. Do you get my point?"

Ted looked at the floor and nodded.

"Now get out of here and do the job I pay you for."

Jack chuckled. *"That boy is too soft. I don't have time to save the world. Full speed ahead, I say, and destroy any son of a bitch who gets in your way."*

❦ ❦ ❦

Later that afternoon Jack heard a knock at his office door.

"Yes, come in."

Ted entered Jack's office, closing the door behind him.

"Excuse me, sir, but something has come up."

"Did you get that Jacksboro problem taken care of?"

"Well, no…not exactly."

"What do you mean, *not exactly*? What is it now?"

"Well, I ah…I offered money to Ed Lomax the city inspector that we've worked with the most."

"Yeah?"

"He wants a lot more money than the last time."

"That greedy bastard," Jack snarled.

"He says because the building is in such good shape, he'll have to grease a lot of palms to get it declared uninhabitable. He says he will have to call in a lot of favors, so it has to be worth his while."

Jack sighed. "All right. How much does he want?"

"Twenty thousand dollars."

"What?" Jack shouted, rising from behind his desk. He was visibly upset. "That's more than double what we paid him the last time."

"What shall I tell him, sir?"

Jack waved his hand dismissively. "Oh, hell. Pay him what he wants. This deal is too big to argue with him about the price."

"Well, unfortunately, that brings up another problem," Ted said.

Growing angrier by the moment, Jack barked, "Now what?"

"Lomax is going on a vacation to Europe in two days. He wants the money by tomorrow morning. Getting twenty thousand dollars that fast won't be easy."

"What are you talking about? This company is a multi-million-dollar organization. All he wants is a measly twenty grand."

"But the bank closes in ten minutes and that amount is too big to cover from one of the petty cash slush funds."

"Yeah, I see what you mean," Jack said. He stared at the ceiling for a few seconds and then an odd light came into his eyes. Snapping his fingers, he said, "I think I know how to fix this. Give me a few minutes. Leave the door open, and send Sandi in on your way out."

As Jack watched Ted walk out of his office,

he thought, *Jack, old man, you're a genius. Pay off Lomax and get rid of bumbling Sandi forever. Brilliant.*

In less than a minute, Sandi entered Jack's office. She looked apprehensive. She assumed she was being called on the carpet for yet another imaginary transgression.

"You wanted to see me, Mr. Crandall?" she asked timidly.

Adopting a friendly tone, Jack waved toward a chair, "Yes, Sandi, sit down. Maybe I've been too hard on you. You've worked for me for a long time, haven't you?"

"Yes, sir," Sandi said, taking a seat in front of Jack's massive desk.

"To show you my heart is in the right place, I want to give you a bonus."

A surprised look crossed Sandi's face. "A bonus?"

"That's right. How does twenty thousand dollars sound?"

Looking overjoyed, she cried, "Oh my! Twenty thousand dollars?"

"Yes, and I want you to have it by tomorrow... you know, before the weekend. So, here's how we are going to do it." He pointed at a steno pad and pen in his secretary's hand.

Sandi flipped open the pad to begin taking notes.

"You'll need to go into the accounting system and transfer twenty thousand dollars from the pension fund to the building and maintenance fund. You got that, Sandi? After you've done the transfer, I want you to draw a check from building and maintenance for twenty thousand dollars. Make it payable to Ed Lomax, L-O-M-A-X and bring it to me."

Sandi stopped writing. A puzzled frown creased her brow. "Who's Ed Lomax?" she asked.

"An old college buddy. He owns a construction company. I've already cleared it with him. He'll cash the check, and I'll give the money to you."

"Cash?" Sandi asked doubtfully.

Jack laughed. "Sandi, I could never get

a bonus of twenty grand past the finance committee. A check to a construction firm from the building and maintenance fund won't be questioned. I have you draw checks like that all the time, don't I? It's the only way I can get you the bonus."

When Sandi hesitated, Jack growled, "Jesus, do you want the money or not? I'm trying to do a nice thing here."

"Well, yes, yes, of course I do. Thank you so much, Mr. Crandall!" Sandi gushed. "But are you sure it's okay to take the money from the pension fund? I was told that account was never to be touched."

"You let me worry about that. I'm authorizing it, and I'll put the money back next week."

Sandi nodded. "Well, I guess if you replace it, then it will be okay. Thank you very much. You've made me so happy!"

"Well, you've earned it. Run along now. And, would you please close the door on your way out."

As soon as she closed the door, Jack dialed Ted's extension. "It's Crandall," he barked. "I'll have a twenty thousand dollar check for Ed Lomax on my desk tomorrow morning."

"How did you…"

"Never mind how. I've got something I want you to do for me."

"Yes, sir?" Ted replied warily.

"You're clever with computers," Jack said, "so here's what I want you to do. Tomorrow, after you pay Lomax, go into the accounting system and find that check. Change the payee from Lomax's name to Sandi's. Can you do that?"

"Oh, Mr. Crandall, I don't know…"

"Are you saying you can't do it?"

Ted stammered, "W…w….well, technically, yes, but it's very illegal. I don't think I should do that, sir. Sandi could go to prison for something like that. It will look like she stole money from the company."

"Yeah, that's the point."

"But, why would you…"

"Ted, how many bribes have you delivered

30

to city building inspectors for me?"

Ted sighed. "A few, I suppose."

"Would you be interested to know that I've had a private investigator secretly video tape and record all of those meetings?"

Ted gasped.

"So, the way I see it, Teddy boy, you either alter the computer records, or those tapes go to the police."

"You wouldn't do that! They make you look just as guilty as they do me, Mr. Crandall. Surely you know that!"

Jack laughed. "The tapes have been edited, you idiot. My name doesn't appear anywhere on them. It looks like the bribes were all your idea. Do you get the picture, Ted? If you're lucky, you might get off with ten years. But, that's only if you get a very sympathetic judge. You have a wife and two rug-rats at home, don't you? So who would you rather see go to prison? You or Sandi?"

After a long silence, Ted said meekly, "I'll change the computer records."

Hanging up the phone, Jack chuckled softly to himself. He thought, *Two birds with one stone. Lomax gets his money, and HR will stop telling me I can't fire Sandi without cause. How is embezzlement for cause? I'll deny that I gave her permission to transfer any funds, and say I have no idea why the twit would write herself a check. I will finally get rid of that stupid pain in the ass for good. I'm truly a genius.*

⚜ ⚜ ⚜

It was a few minutes before seven o'clock that evening when Jacks doorbell rang. When he opened the door, there stood a chauffeur. He was splendidly dressed in a crisp uniform, his cap tucked neatly under his arm.

"I guess you must be the driver from the West Side Dining Club." Jack gave him the once over.

"Yes, sir. My name is George. This way to your car, please."

In the driveway sat a Rolls Royce Silver Cloud limousine. It was immaculate.

Jacks eyes grew wide. He whistled. "Wow, quite a car."

"Yes sir, it is."

George opened the door for Jack. After he was comfortably settled in the_rear seat, the chauffeur walked around and took his place behind the wheel. The limo started with a soft purr and pulled out of Jack's driveway. Jack thought it strange that George kept the headlights off until they were more than a block from his house, but in his excitement, he soon forgot about it.

"So, George, you're Mr. Maricopa's chauffeur?" Jack asked.

"No, Mr. Crandall, I'm a member of the dining club. We have no paid staff, so we all pitch in where we can."

"You drive all the guests to dinner each year?"

"Yes sir, for the past eighteen years."

"I guess you must have driven some pretty important people."

The driver's eyes met Jack's in the rearview mirror. "Why, all of our guests are important, Mr. Crandall."

"Anyone I might have heard of?"

"Sorry, I'm not allowed to say."

"Oh, come on, pal. What could it hurt?"

"I really can't, Mr. Crandall. Rules, you know. We're not much for publicity."

"Yeah, I gathered that. How much longer?"

"Not long, just a few minutes."

As they drove, Jack noticed they were heading deeper into one of the seedier parts of town.

True to his word, in only a few minutes George pulled into an alley behind a building. It appeared to be an abandoned warehouse. As the Rolls came to a stop, a narrow door opened, and a man dressed in a tuxedo stepped toward the car.

Opening the door of the limo, the man extended his hand. "Ah, Mr. Crandall, it's so nice to meet you."

"You must be Mr. Maricopa," Jack said,

shaking the offered hand.

"Yes. I trust the ride was enjoyable?"

"Yeah, I should say so. Don't see too many Rolls Royce limos around." Taking in the dimly lit alley, he added, "This building isn't quite what I was expecting, though."

"This way, sir." Maricopa gestured for Jack to follow him. "As I explained on the phone, we try to keep a low profile."

"It's low alright," Jack replied. "I know just about everyone in this town, and I've never heard of you or the West Side Dining Club before."

Maricopa led Jack up a flight of rickety stairs. George followed behind.

"No elevator?" Jack asked.

Maricopa shook his head. "To the passerby, this building appears to be an abandoned warehouse. An elevator wouldn't be in keeping with that illusion."

Illusion? Jack thought.

"Here we are. Please have a seat and make yourself at home." Maricopa waved expansively toward the room.

"May I take your coat, Mr. Crandall?" George offered. Removing his coat, Jack took in his amazing surroundings. No expense had been spared in making everything look warm, plush and inviting. He took a seat on a velvet sofa before a massive stone fireplace, ablaze with crackling logs.

"Wow," Jack exclaimed. "I've been in every private club in this town, and none of them are as nice as this. You must have spent a fortune on this room alone."

"We've spared no expense. We want our guests to enjoy their stay with us." Maricopa smiled.

Jack looked puzzled. "Hey, pal, this just doesn't add up. How is it that I've never heard of you? You operate out of the fanciest place in town, but you want the outside to look…well… you mentioned something about an illusion. What's going on here?"

"In due time, Mr. Crandall, in due time. All of our guests have had similar questions. You'll have answers before the night is over."

George appeared with a silver tray. "Champagne, gentlemen?" he asked.

"Ah," Maricopa rubbed his hands together. "Here's the champagne, now." He handed a crystal flute to Jack.

Taking a sip, Jack smacked his lips. "Mmmmmm…this is great! Outstanding!" he said, raising the glass in a mock toast.

"I thought you'd find it to your liking."

"How long has the club been open, Mr. Maricopa?"

"Well, we've never actually been open in the normal sense, but we have been in existence for eighty-seven years."

"But you haven't ah…I mean you aren't that old…"

Maricopa chuckled. "No, Mr. Crandall. I've been personally associated with the club for thirty-one years. And I have served as president for the last twelve."

"How did the club find you?" Jack asked.

"Membership is passed from generation to generation. My father was a member, and my grandfather was the original founder of the club."

"So, you have to be born into it?"

"That's correct."

"Who are the rest of the members?" Jack asked.

"They come from some of the more prominent families in the city. They'll see you at dinner, Mr. Crandall." Maricopa said dismissively.

Jack shrugged. "And all this is just so you can honor some poor slob at dinner once a year?"

"Yes. That's why we're here."

"I don't get it, but it's your money, Maricopa. Am I supposed to say a few words during the meal? I mean, is that what they're expecting? I didn't prepare anything."

"Ah, no. That won't be necessary."

"Now what's this illusion you were talking about?" Jack questioned.

"Oh, it's no mystery, really. Because of the

32

prominence of some of our members, we like to keep our activities quiet. So, we make the front of the building look inconspicuous. The less people know about us, the better."

"I guess that makes sense. So, obviously, you know a lot more about me than I do about your club."

"Yes, Mr. Crandall, we've followed your career for years."

"Really?" Jack grinned. He was clearly flattered. "Then I guess you know, not everyone in town likes me?"

"Yes, we are aware. How do you feel about that?"

"How do I feel about it? I really don't care what people think. To hell with 'em, I say. I got where I am today by working hard and taking no prisoners. If I had to do it all over again, I'd do it exactly the same way."

Maricopa grimaced. "Is that right? Nothing you would change?"

Jack shook his head. "Nope. So, tell me, Maricopa, since this club has been around for eighty-seven years, does that mean I'm your eighty-seventh guest?"

"Indeed, you are, Mr. Crandall. We have entertained only one guest per year from the very beginning."

"Why only one dinner a year?" Jack asked.

"It just seems to work out best that way," was Maricopa's elusive reply.

"Will any of your past guests be joining us tonight?"

Maricopa shook his head. "No, I'm afraid none of them could make it this evening."

"Too bad," Jack said. "So, since you picked me to honor at this year's dinner, you must like the way I do things."

Maricopa looked as though he had just tasted something bitter, as he replied, "Not exactly, Mr. Crandall. The truth is, we despise everything about you."

"Yeah, right," Jack laughed. "Rolls Royce, expensive champagne. You're quite a joker, Maricopa. You said so yourself, I was chosen for this dinner because of my accomplishments."

"No, I'm not joking, Mr. Crandall. And as for your accomplishments…well, I must admit, that was a bit of a lie."

Jack glared at the man with a puzzled frown.

Maricopa continued, "Actually, you were chosen because of the ruthless way you went about garnering those accomplishments."

"What the hell are you talking about?" Jack asked, starting to grow nervous.

"Mr. Crandall, when you asked if I was aware that some people in this town don't like you, you were in error. We couldn't find anyone in this entire town who likes you. Many were afraid of you, but none had a single kind word to say."

"Now, just a minute," Jack protested.

"They don't like you because you've utilized every dishonest method you could to get what you wanted," Maricopa explained. "You use people and then discard them when they're no longer of value to you. You've ruined countless lives and were the direct cause of at least four suicides. You lie, cheat and steal at will. We've investigated you thoroughly, Mr. Crandall, and we couldn't find that you possess even the smallest redeeming feature."

"Wait a minute, I don't have to take this shit and I…"

"But the crowning glory— what really influenced my vote for you, is the vile, mean, and inhumane way you've treated your secretary for years."

"Sandi?" Jack asked in surprise. "What do you know about Sandi?"

"I know a great deal about her. You see, she's my niece. In fact, it was Sandi who first brought you to our attention several years back."

Anger showed in Jack's voice as he snarled, "That bitch set me up."

"No," Maricopa assured him. "She's a niece by marriage. She's not a member of the club, and she knows nothing about tonight. She did call me earlier today, however. She was apprehensive about the cash bonus you offered her. I advised her not to perform that bit of accounting you asked her to do, and to request her bonus be paid by check—one signed by you. I believe it was Sandi who was being set up, Mr. Crandall."

Jack glared at Maricopa incredulously. "I don't understand. You invited me to be the guest of honor at the only dinner you're giving this year. You must have seen something you liked."

"Well, I did promise you some answers, didn't I? You see, Mr. Crandall, my grandfather started this club after returning from a South American expedition, where he was captured by a fierce tribe and nearly lost his life. He's the only known man to be captured by this native tribe and live to tell about it. For some reason they took a liking to him, and he lived with them for eighteen months before returning to the United States. Upon his return, he founded this club with two purposes in mind: fine dining, and an expedient way to rid the world of undesirables—like yourself."

"That's it. I'm getting the hell out of here," Jack snarled. "I don't have to take this."

Maricopa shook his head regretfully. "I'm afraid there's no time for you to go anywhere, Mr. Crandall." He glanced at his watch. "You'll be dead in less than two minutes. You see, the champagne you drank contained a colorless, odorless, and quite deadly poison. My grandfather discovered it while in South America. All trace of it leaves the body within five minutes after death."

"My God, that's murder," Jack screamed. "What kind of person are you that would invite a man to be your dinner guest and then kill him?"

Maricopa sighed. "Why, I thought by now you'd understand. You're not our dinner guest, Mr. Crandall. You're the main course. Quite a delicacy! Now perhaps you understand what I meant when I said we were looking forward to serving you tonight."

A look of horror crossed Jack's face as the full weight of what Maricopa had just told him began to sink in. "The main course?" he said in a whisper, barely getting the words out.

"My grandfather was captured by a tribe of cannibals. In the year and a half that he stayed with them, he not only grew to love them, he also grew quite fond of their diet. Upon his return, he passed that taste on to his family, and to the families of a few very close friends. They, in turn, passed it down through the generations. Each club member is a descendant of one of those families."

"You're insane! You won't get away with this. I'm going to stand up right now, walk out of here, go to a hospital and then to the police…. and…. oh God…….ooohhhhhhhhh…."

Jack's eyes rolled back in his head and he slowly slumped to the floor.

Looking down at Jack's body, George stepped gingerly over him. He turned to Maricopa. "I'll take Mr. Crandall into the kitchen now and start the preparations."

Maricopa began to chuckle softly. "Fine, George. He didn't understand until the very end, did he? And after I'd told him several times how much we were looking forward to serving him. I've only seen one guest who was more surprised."

George smiled, remembering fondly. "You mean Jimmy Hoffa?"

"Yes, George, Mr. Hoffa."

Ken Kreps is a writer, actor, acting coach, and casting director. He has written several audio plays for the radio anthology series, "Imagination Theater". He has also written many screenplays, short stories, articles, and essays.

As an actor, he has appeared in "The Office" on NBC, Hulu's first scripted series, and several independent films and commercials. Ken was the casting director for "The Right Way" by Tom Kennedy, which was released in 2014.

Raised in San Antonio, Texas, Ken graduated Sul Ross University in West Texas with a degree in music. He was a professional jazz trombonist for a number of years. Ken also served in The United States Air Force.

An Uninvited Guest

by Catherine Turner

Hell is empty and all the devils are here.
-William Shakespeare

EMILY GLANCED NERVOUSLY around the room. She bit her lower lip as she watched the minutes tick by on the clock above the stove. She fought the urge to open the oven door, knowing one wrong move and the soufflé would collapse like a sapling in a hailstorm.

Her guests would arrive at seven for dinner. Emily reminded herself to keep her facial expressions in check when the Millers' arrived. There could be no eye rolls, no smirks and no grimaces regardless of how much Elaine's fawning over Dex annoyed her.

The guest list was a colorful one. She had invited Carrie—or as everyone now referred to her, *Poor Carrie*, more out of a sense of obligation than any real desire for her company. Carrie had sacrificed the last ten years of her life to keep her mother out of one of those dreadful institutions, no matter how advanced the dementia got. It was only now, since her mother had wandered away from home and gotten lost twice while Carrie was at work, that she was starting to face the inevitable. She could not afford to have a caregiver stay with the elderly woman on a daily basis, and she was finding it impossible to continue caring for her mother by herself.

Carting around excess weight, her pretty years behind her, Carrie had grown resentful of her thinner and freer friends in recent years. While she wasn't much fun to have at these gatherings anymore, it would have been cruel to leave her off the guest list. They had been friends for a long time.

Celeste and Paul Beaumont were coming too. Inviting them felt the same way Emily imagined prosecutors felt when they call a witness to the stand who could either make or break their entire case, and they aren't really sure which way it will go once they get them up there. They could only hope for the best. Those witnesses were known as *Wild Cards*.

If the Beaumont's hadn't started drinking before their arrival, and they were getting along well, they would be the life of the party—they always were. If, however, they were in the middle of one of their legendary arguments, you should brace yourself for a food fight. They were a rather volatile couple. A *Wild Card* couple, one might say.

Paul had made his money managing a few hedge funds. Not all of his trading was entirely legal, but the more money he made, the more Celeste spent, and she had grown accustomed to the lifestyle.

Of course, Emily wasn't one to judge. Before his untimely passing, Emily's husband Rob hadn't always made clean money either, and with her mini-mansion paid off and an expensive European import parked in the garage, she wasn't about to throw stones.

She glanced at the clock again. Two minutes left. Preparing to handle the soufflé with the delicacy of a bomb squad deactivating a dangerous incendiary device, she donned oven mitts and gingerly approached the stove. As she reached to open the oven the doorbell rang.

"Ugh. You gotta be kidding me!" she muttered to herself. Her guests weren't due to start arriving for another half hour, so who had ignored social protocol and shown up early? *Must be Carrie,* she thought. Her mother had been driving her crazy this week. She probably escaped the moment the in-home nurse pulled into her driveway.

Oven mitts still on, Emily raced to open the door. She had just over a minute to let the early arriving guest inside and race back to the kitchen with the speed of a gazelle.

Expecting to see Carrie's sad moon-face on the other side of the door, Emily gasped when she was met with an older gentleman. He looked quite dapper in a handsome black suit, and his blue eyes twinkled under salt and pepper eyebrows. He removed a bowler from his head and bowed.

"Good Evening, Mrs. Marston," he said pleasantly. He noted the oven gloves and said, "Oh, dear, it looks like I have come at a bad time... but of course, there really is no good time for business such as this, now is there?"

Despite his cheerful demeanor, something about this man frightened her. Removing the oven mitts, her soufflé forgotten for the moment, Emily said, "I'm sorry, but you're right, this really isn't a good time. If you are selling something, the neighborhood doesn't allow solicitors, so I will need to ask you to leave."

The man chuckled and shook his head. "Allow me to introduce myself. I am Mr. Eternity. Pleased to make your acquaintance." He grasped Emily's hand and held it firmly when she tried to extract it from his grip.

Emily thought, *Uh-oh, he must be crazy like Carrie's mom! Probably wandered away from home and can't find his way back. Only this one seems a hell of a lot more dangerous than a harmless little old lady. What the hell do I do now?*

The soufflé was burning. She could smell it.

"I...I have to get something out of the oven, it's burning. I really have to go. Do you live around here? Is there someone I can call for you?"

The man shocked the hell out of Emily when he said, "I'm terribly sorry about your soufflé, Mrs. Marston. This is all my fault. Here, maybe I can fix it." He marched past her and into the house.

Emily gave a startled squawk. She was too shocked to move for a few seconds. How the hell did he know it was a soufflé she had in the oven? Ungluing her feet from the floor just as the stranger entered her kitchen, Emily ran to catch up with him. He sure moved fast. He was reaching for the oven door just as Emily flew into the kitchen. Seeing him reach into the oven with his bare hands, Emily screamed, "No! Don't do that! It's ho..." her voice trailed off as the man picked up the soufflé with the gentleness of a mother handling a newborn baby and laid it on top of the stove. He waved a hand over the top of the soufflé and Emily watched as the top transformed from a charred, unappetizing black, to a perfect cocoa hue.

He turned back to look at Emily, and said, "See? All better. Not burned at all. It's perfect."

Emily sagged against the polished granite of her kitchen counter. She stared at the soufflé and then shifted her eyes to the stranger in her house with an expression of mingled horror and amazement. "How, how did you... why aren't you burned? What the hell is going on here? Who are you?"

"As I said, my name is "Mr. Eternity. I think that sounds so much more pleasant than my other monikers— The Grim Reaper, for instance. The Angel of Death is another of my more distasteful names. In any event, I am here because it's time for another soul, and your number is up Emily."

An icy shiver of fear climbed Emily's back as she stared wide-eyed at the man. She began back-peddling for the living room, then turned and ran. She screamed when she rounded the corner and slammed into the stranger. Somehow he had beaten her out of the kitchen even though she had a running head start, and he was now standing between her and the doorway. If she could just survive this nightmare for twenty more minutes her friends would arrive and rescue her. Right now twenty minutes felt like an eternity. She did not know how in the hell this lunatic managed to pick up the soufflé with his bare hands and not pay for the feat with third degree burns, and right now she didn't care. She just wanted to get him out of her house.

"Listen, I have money. If it's money you want, just tell me how much!" she cried desperately.

"You aren't listening, and we don't have much time. I am here to offer you a deal. A once in a lifetime proposal, really."

Emily looked at him, ever mindful that the longer she stalled him, the closer she was to someone arriving and putting an end to this madness. She nodded. "Okay, what's the deal? I'm listening."

"I said it's time for another soul, but it doesn't necessarily have to be yours. I am willing to trade your life for one of your guests tonight."

Emily's jaw dropped open in shock. She stammered, "You want to kill me or one of my friends, is that what you are saying? Are you insane?"

The man sighed in frustration. He muttered, "They never get this part. Why are mortals so stupid?" He shook his head and said, "No, Mrs. Marston, or may I call you Emily? This has nothing to do with what I want. The simple fact is, one of you will die tonight, and you must decide who it will be."

"I don't understand what..."

He cut her off, "And by the way, I will be staying for dinner, so you may want to add another place setting to your lovely table."

Emily felt dizzy. She sat down hard on the couch. "Why do you think someone here is going to die tonight? That's crazy. You realize that, don't you?"

"Oh my, time is running out. Who would you like me to be for your guests? Perhaps I should be your Cousin Billy? He's your Aunt Helen's boy, if I'm not mistaken. All your friends have heard of him, right? You made him up so you would have an alibi when you run off on one of your rendezvous' with your friend Elaine's husband. When you leave town you tell everyone you are going to bail Billy out of jail or help him out of a jam."

Emily gasped in shock. She felt like she had just been slapped across the face. This was one corner of her life absolutely no one knew about.

Before Emily could even begin to recover from the intruder's stinging, and painfully accurate accusation, he transformed before her very eyes. He was suddenly no longer a dapper old man in a suit. Standing before her now was a tall, lean man in his mid-forties with a long, graying pony tail, a leather vest and jeans. Across his right knuckles was a tattoo of the name *Vicki*. Another tattoo of a dragon crawled from the collar of his shirt.

He said, "Look out the window, Emily. There is imaginary Cousin Billy's motorcycle. You could say I showed up unexpectedly."

Emily cried, "How did you..."

"Or, maybe you would rather I was Billy's mother, Aunt Helen."

Suddenly, with dizzying speed he changed again. Now Emily was looking at an old woman with carefully coifed hair with a salon blue rinse. She wore a stiff floral dress, cheap pearls and bifocals. When Emily glanced out the window, the motorcycle was gone. It had been replaced by an aging blue sedan.

Emily's face turned the color of cheese. Her breath was coming in shallow, little gasps, and she felt on the verge of a faint. "You aren't real. I imagined you. I fell asleep and I am dreaming. Something! Anything! This is not happening." She shook her head violently back and forth and pinched her eyes shut. "When I open my eyes you will be gone."

"I suggest you try and get it together, Emily. We only have about ten minutes before our guests arrive. Okay, Billy it is," he said decisively

and turned back into the middle-aged biker.

Emily opened her eyes. Seeing the intruder was still before her, she yelled, "No! You don't understand. Dex knows I made Cousin Billy up. The others think he's real, but Dex knows he isn't. He will have a million questions."

"I wouldn't worry too much about Dexter, Emily. He will have a full plate this evening just trying to keep his own secrets, I suspect. Having your wife and your mistress at the same dinner table requires a certain amount of finesse. It should keep him sufficiently occupied."

"Don't call him Dexter," Emily warned.

The man who had taken over the identity of her imaginary cousin smirked. "Ah, yes. He prefers 'Dex' doesn't he? Thinks it sounds sexier than his given name of Dexter."

Emily nodded. "No one calls him that, he hates it."

"No more time for idle chatter. It's time for you to make your decision. Who at tonight's dinner table will you choose?"

Emily looked at him blankly. "I can't," she moaned. "You know I can't do what you ask. Why me?"

"Why you?" he laughed. "Do you think your life has been blameless? You don't think you deserve this?"

"What are you talking about?" Emily asked, truly baffled. "Is this about me and Dex?"

"Do you remember a gentleman by the name of Arthur Benson?"

Emily gasped. "Oh my God! I haven't thought of him in years."

"Well, do you remember stealing his credit card and then blackmailing him with photos of the two of you together? Didn't you threaten to send them to his wife if he didn't allow you to keep the card and use it to your heart's content? What was the name of that club where you were a dancer, Emily?"

"The Kitten Club," Emily replied absently. "Jesus, that was over thirty years ago and I was dead broke. I used the poor sap's card to pay my damn rent. I wasn't out shoe shopping, you know."

"Well, poor Arthur succumbed to a heart attack six months later. Might it have been all the stress you caused? It doesn't matter how long ago it was, all sins must be atoned for sooner or later."

Emily drew a shaking hand across her brow and swiped at a tear sliding down her cheek. "What are you?" she asked, "The devil? Are you Satan?"

"Not exactly. You could say he's my employer, I suppose."

Emily looked incredulous. "And he sent you to me? Why not an axe murderer, or a serial killer or something? Forgive me, but next to some people I am a saint."

"Do you remember Carla Gentry?"

Emily threw her hands up in a warding off gesture and jumped up from the couch. "Don't you dare blame me for Carla! I had nothing to do with that! If you think I was involved then your boss has been feeding you wrong information."

He shrugged. "Maybe you weren't, but your late husband, well that's another story. Miss Gentry found out what he was up to and she disappeared right before she could blow the whistle. Would you like me to tell you where she is now?"

"No!" Emily shrieked. "No! I don't care! Leave me alone. I barely knew her. She was my husband's secretary for a few short months, and if Rob did something to her, then go find him wherever he is now. Leave me out of this. I am not paying for the sins of my dead husband."

Emily was starting to feel like she was in the middle of some twisted version of *A Christmas Carol* and all the visitors were the Ghosts of Christmas Past. This Mr. Eternity, as he called himself, was bringing things up she hadn't thought about in years, and they were things she would rather never think about again— particularly the disappearance of Carla Gentry.

On the day Rob died, or more correctly, on the day Rob staged his suicide to look like an accident, he left her a note with a box of matches sitting beside it on the kitchen counter. The note instructed her to burn after reading. The jig was up, it said. The grand jury was getting ready to hand down a formal indictment against him.

The Securities and Exchange Commission had been breathing fire down Rob's neck for months. He had grown increasingly more desperate. Emily knew it was possible he believed getting rid of Carla, the star witness against him, would solve all his problems. Emily never knew for sure if he was responsible for the woman's disappearance. Rob never actually told her he was involved, but the timing was certainly suspect.

With Carla gone and the heat still turned all the way up, Rob decided to check out before the hammer fell by staging a car accident. He transferred most of his money to offshore accounts so Emily wouldn't lose everything. He left the passbooks with his incriminating suicide note—which Emily did indeed burn after reading, as instructed. He told her that the million dollars in life insurance would sustain her until enough time had passed for her to access the offshore accounts where the rest of the money was hidden. He said on the ten year anniversary of his death she would be safe to start using that money. *Only a little at a time*, he warned. The ten year anniversary of Rob's death was next week.

Mr. Eternity, or let's just call him Cousin Billy for now, interrupted Emily's reminiscing. He stood up and said, "I need a name now, Emily. The first guests are arriving. Either give me the name of who will die in your stead, or I will take your soul right now."

He raised the first two fingers of his left hand and two sizzling beams of blue light shot from them like small lightning bolts. He aimed them at Emily's face and she took an involuntary step backward and raised her hands defensively.

"Alright! Stop it! I will do it! I will give you a name, just get that thing away from me," she sobbed.

The doorbell rang and Emily pulled in a

40

long, shuddering breath.

The imaginary cousin she had conjured up as an alibi to cover her misdeeds sighed. "Get the door Emily. You can give me the name after your guests leave. But, I warn you, if you breathe one word to any of them about my true identity, I will take every last one of their souls tonight and the devil will be very pleased."

"I won't!" Emily gasped, "Please don't hurt anyone!"

"And remember, this is a binding contract. You have agreed to trade your own soul for one of your guests. In exchange I will let you live, and will even help you serve the appetizers." He smiled gleefully. "Now go clean up. Your makeup is all runny." With that he disappeared into the kitchen.

Emily staggered a little as she walked to the foyer and checked her appearance in a wall mirror hanging near the door. She hastily smoothed her hair and wiped the mascara streak from her cheek.

Arranging her face into what she hoped was a smile, she flung open the front door with a shaking hand. She was greeted by Celeste and Paul Beaumont.

"What took you so long, sweetie? It's freezing out here. I need a martini to warm me up," Celeste said, planting air-kisses on both sides of Emily's cheeks.

"Whose bike is that?" Paul asked, hooking a thumb in the direction of the street. "Sweet ride."

"Why, thank you," Billy called heartily, with a slight southern drawl. He strode into the living room carrying a tray with two martini glasses and some finger foods.

"Well, who do we have here?" Celeste asked, dropping a wink in Emily's direction. "Never took you for the biker boy kind, my dear."

Emily gasped. "No! It's not that. He isn't..."

Billy cut her off. "I'm Emily's cousin. I dropped in on her unannounced today on my way through town and she was kind enough to invite me to stay for dinner. Nice to meet you folks." He extended a hand to Paul.

"I'm Paul and this is my wife Celeste."

"My name's Billy. May I take your coat, Celeste?"

Unbuttoning her shiny quilted coat, Celeste cried, "Oh my God! You're Billy? *Thee* Billy? Aunt Helen's boy, right? We've been hearing about you for years!"

Emily wasn't surprised to see Celeste wearing a mini-skirt and thigh-high boots. Most of her wardrobe was attire much more appropriate to a woman half her age. Of course, Celeste still had the figure to pull it off.

Billy handed Paul one of the martinis and took Celeste's coat. The two men walked into the house talking about his motorcycle.

Celeste sipped her drink and looked at Emily with a critical eye. "Are you okay? You don't look so good."

Emily smiled. "Thank you, darling. You flatter me."

"Sorry, babe. No offense, you just look white as a sheet. Are you sick or something?"

"Just a touch of the flu. I'm fine." Emily shrugged it off.

"The flu, really?" Celeste asked skeptically. "You were fine yesterday when you whipped my ass on the tennis court."

"It's nothing, Celeste. Just a bug I caught last night." She was saved from more of Celeste's probing questions by a knock at the door.

Soon all her guests had arrived and were settled around the living room with appetizers and drinks. They chatted comfortably and introductions were made. Everyone seemed fascinated with Cousin Billy—especially Dex.

Emily excused herself to the kitchen to get dinner ready. Once alone in the kitchen, she stood in front of the sink and hung her head. A shudder wracked her shoulders and she gripped the counter with both hands. Her mind wandered to the strange, uninvited guest who was laughing and entertaining her friends. He had picked up the soufflé from a scorching oven with his bare hands, and somehow removed the charred mess it had become and turned it into a dessert worthy of a king. He had literally shape-shifted right before her eyes from a dapper old man, to a biker, and then to an old woman, complete with bifocals and pearls. Not to mention the vehicles he conjured up outside.

He said he wasn't the devil, but Emily couldn't kid herself. He obviously wasn't human either. She was in big trouble and she didn't want to believe the only way out of it was to sacrifice one of her friends to him.

A pair of arms encircled Emily's waist from behind and she jumped and stifled a scream. Nuzzling her neck, Dex said, "Easy, Em. It's just me."

"You scared me half to death. I didn't hear you come in." She leaned back against him.

Then came the inevitable question. "So who is that guy? I thought you didn't really have a Cousin Billy."

She smiled up at him. "Well, tonight I do. So just let it go, okay?"

Voices were heard approaching and Dex hastily let go of Emily's waist and stepped a few feet back from the sink.

The conversation at the dinner table flowed easily around Emily. The star of the show was of course, Cousin Billy, who regaled them with tales of bar-fights, getting tangled up with a Mexican drug cartel, incarceration, and Vicki; the lady whose name was tattooed across his knuckles. Emily wasn't surprised to see Celeste flirting with him. She also didn't miss Dex's puzzled expression as he looked back and forth between herself and the cousin who Dex believed to be a figment of her imagination until tonight.

At one point she felt an odd wave of affection for her uninvited guest when he told Carrie, "Darlin' I think I'll tattoo your name across the back of my other hand."

Carrie blushed to the roots of her hair and giggled like a schoolgirl. It was good to see her happy. Then Emily reminded herself that Cousin Billy was actually a monster in a leather vest, and if it was Carrie's name she gave him at

the end of the evening, he wouldn't hesitate to kill her friend. The warm fuzzy feeling dissolved instantly.

Once the meal was eaten, Emily asked Billy to freshen everyone's drinks. She excused herself to put up a pot of coffee and get dessert.

Dex rose from the table and said, "I'll help you clear." He began picking up plates.

Elaine laughed and said, "Gee, why can't I get you to do that at home?"

Even in these strange circumstances, Emily had to fight not to roll her eyes.

"Oh," Celeste quipped, "Come on Elaine, we all know you have Dex trained better than your Golden Retriever."

Great, Emily thought, *let the drunken chatter begin.*

Emily managed to dodge Dex's questions about who the mystery man really was.

"If the guy is real," he asked, "Why wouldn't you just tell me?"

She smiled and replied, "Can't a girl have a few secrets?"

Dex shrugged. "Sure, but why lie about this?"

Emily busied herself with coffee and dessert plates. She slapped a corkscrew into Dex's hands and asked him to open another bottle of wine. Given how much everyone, including herself, had already had to drink, this probably wasn't advisable, but seemed the only way to get him out of the kitchen and stop his endless questions about Cousin Billy.

Everyone raved about the chocolate soufflé. It was cooked to perfection. The meal had been a success. Once everyone was settled in the living room with nightcaps and coffee, eventually the conversation began to lag, and hands were raised to stifle yawns. It was time to call it a night.

While Emily still had no idea what she was going to do about the deal she had entered into with her strange visitor, for some reason she wasn't scared anymore. An eerie sense of calm had replaced her earlier terror. She suspected that had more to do with the wine she drank than anything else.

She watched everyone hug Cousin Billy and gush about how wonderful it had been to meet him. Then Billy slipped away and left Emily to see her guests out.

She told Carrie to text her when she got home and told everyone else to drive safely. She stood at the door and watched her friends get into their vehicles and drive away. She wondered if they were all going to live through the night. She wondered the same thing about herself. The words to an old song by Thin Lizzy floated through her mind; *Drinks will flow and blood will spill.* She closed the front door hoping with all her heart there would be no prophecy to those words tonight.

Emily went to the dining room and was surprised to find the table clear of dishes. Only the last bit of chocolate soufflé remained in the middle. Emily spooned it into a dish and poured herself another glass of wine. She carried them into the kitchen, and was further surprised to see her strange, uninvited guest loading the dishwasher. He was humming the tune to *The Boys are Back in Town,* the same song Emily had just been thinking about the lyrics to. She wasn't surprised.

She was curious why he was still in his Cousin Billy persona. She thought once the guests were gone he would have switched back to the gentleman who greeted her at the door wearing a bowler hat. He was certainly a great deal more frightening in that incarnation than he was as Cousin Billy.

She pulled out a stool from underneath the island and sat down to eat the soufflé and drink the wine. Her guest seemed content to be doing the dishes.

Emily remarked, "Still Cousin Billy, huh? You like playing that role, I think."

He smiled. "Well, it's not very often I get to be a bad-ass, as the kids call it. I must say it's been quite fun."

Emily rolled her eyes. "Oh please, you're on Satan's payroll. It doesn't get much more bad-ass

than that."

He laughed and pointed at the spoonful of soufflé she was raising to her lips. "Came out perfect, just like I promised. Can I let you in on a little secret?"

"Sure"

"I fixed the Beef Wellington too. If you don't mind my saying so, it was a little overcooked." He dropped a conspiratorial wink.

"Gee thanks," she said dryly, "You're a regular Julia Child."

Once the dishwasher was loaded, he dried his hands on a dishtowel and turned to face Emily. He said simply, "It's time."

Emily looked at him and said nothing.

"Look, I know this isn't easy for you, so why don't you write the name down of whose soul you wish me to take in lieu of yours on a piece of paper and give it to me. That way you won't have to say the name out loud. Okay? You see, I am not without some compassion."

Emily sighed and rose from the stool. "Yeah, you're a real prince." She walked into the living room and rummaged through a small antique desk in the corner of the room. Extracting a pad of paper and a pen, she sat on the couch and pulled her legs up underneath her.

The strange guest who had just washed all of her dinner dishes, and now wanted someone's soul, stood across the room from her in front of the fireplace. He turned his back on her and began rubbing his hands together in front of the fire.

"I wonder who it will be," he said more to himself than Emily. "Maybe Carrie? She's had such a sad life since her mother took ill. Or maybe Elaine? Then you could have Dex all to yourself—though, I suspect you don't really want that. I think part of the allure of that relationship is the danger of getting caught."

He moved on to Celeste, and Emily tuned out his monologue and began writing. When she finished she folded the piece of paper and held it out between two fingers. She said nothing.

Finally he turned from the fireplace and

saw her holding out the piece of paper to him. "Excellent!" he cried and clapped his hands together.

He plucked the paper from her outstretched fingers and unfolded it with an almost lustful expression. Staring at what she had written for a long moment, the good humor drained from his face.

Shaking his head, he said, "No, Emily, it doesn't work that way." He let go of the paper and it fluttered to the floor at his feet. He was trying to sound ominous, but Emily thought she saw fear flash in his eyes when he looked at the name on the paper.

He pointed to the pad and pen on the table before her and growled through clenched teeth, "You have five seconds to write down another name, or I will strike you dead where you sit. Do you understand me?"

Emily crossed her arms over her chest and slowly shook her head back and forth. While he stubbornly remained Cousin Billy, she felt no fear of him. She could not understand why he still wasn't changing his appearance—especially now that she had defied him. Had he done that, she might have been scared enough to obey him. But he didn't, so she left the pad of paper sitting before her untouched.

Suddenly the room felt like it dropped twenty degrees and a cold wind began to blow inside the house. Emily gasped as her curtains fluttered in the arctic draft. A thick tendril of black smoke blew into the room and headed directly toward her visitor. He cringed and backed up into the corner.

"Oh no. Now you've done it. He's going to incinerate us both!" he barked at Emily.

She could see that he was utterly terrified. She watched in awe as the smoke grew into a huge towering black shadow in front of her fireplace. It was opaque enough to see the fire blazing behind it. Then it transformed into the shape of a monster that dwarfed the man cowering in the corner. While it remained just a black shadow, there were two malevolent ruby

red eyes blazing from its head. Emily could see a pair of twisted and misshapen horns growing from its forehead and vampire fangs, easily five inches in length, protruding from its mouth. She drew her legs up and buried her face in her hands.

The frightened man began babbling, "I'm sorry, Master. I will fix it. I promise you, Master. Please, I..."

The demon spoke, and Emily thought he sounded exactly like Darth Vader. "Silence," it commanded.

The babbling stopped at once.

The famous line from Star Wars, "Luke, I am your father," raced through Emily's mind and she stifled hysterical laughter with a fist pressed against her lips. *I wonder if the devil knows he sounds exactly like James Earl Jones,* she wondered and then scolded herself for having Dex open that final bottle of wine.

"You imbecile. You have been bested by a mortal," the monster roared in that weird thunderous electronic voice.

It was scary as hell, but Emily thought she heard amusement as well as anger when it spoke.

The paper on which Emily had written the name of whose soul she chose to sacrifice suddenly burst into flames in the middle of the living room floor. The laughter dried up in her throat.

"No, Master, I can..."

"I said silence!"

The man whimpered and then fell quiet.

"You could not just come here and take the human's soul, could you? No, you had to play one of your foolish little games, and now the mortal has won. She fulfilled her end of the agreement, and I have lost my new soul."

The name that Emily had written on the paper was, of course, *Cousin Billy.* Below it she had written, *Aunt Helen's boy.* And below that she scribbled, *Billy has a girlfriend named Vicki. Her name is tattooed on his hand.*

She wasn't sure what compelled her to add those details, but it occurred to her that while she

44

might have been the one who originally created him, it was Mr. Eternity who made Cousin Billy real. He gave him an identity, complete with tattoos, a past, a girlfriend, and even a Harley Davidson motorcycle parked at the curb. He clearly loved being Cousin Billy much more than he did Mr. Eternity. Maybe that's why the Cousin Billy persona still did not have a hair out of place. Maybe he had taken things too far and he couldn't change back anymore.

He said the shadow demon would incinerate them both, but that towering, smoky silhouette didn't seem very interested in Emily. In fact it hadn't even acknowledged she was in the room. That was just fine with her.

The shadow began to waver and then blew into tendrils of long smoke again. It began wafting toward her front door. Emily jumped off the couch and raced to the foyer. She flung open the door seconds before the smoke reached it. The last tendrils formed a loop that wrapped around Cousin Billy's head. He was unceremoniously yanked toward the front door by his ear.

Emily watched in wonder as the black smoke propelled him outside. Once they were beyond her porch light it was too dark for her to see the smoke any longer, but she could see Cousin Billy being flung onto his motorcycle. His hands slapped down on the handlebars and the bike roared to life. She heard him scream and saw him lift his feet off the ground bare seconds before the bike squealed from the curb and zoomed down the street at an impossible rate of speed.

Emily ran to the curb and watched the motorcycle as it raced into the intersection at the corner of her street, never even slowing down to heed the stop sign there. It ended up right in the path of an oncoming SUV. She covered her ears when she heard the stomach dropping screech of brakes, immediately followed by a horrific crash of metal meeting metal. Emily watched in terror as the motorcycle was launched into the air. It landed on its side with a bone-rattling crunch, and what looked like a large ragdoll pinned beneath it.

Amazingly the wreckage was still moving. It was now a deformed hunk of steel sliding back down the street toward Emily's house with a deafening squeal and sparks flying from beneath it.

The twisted mass of metal and the ragdoll finally came to rest across the street, directly under the glare of an illuminated street lamp. Emily moaned when she saw a lone motorcycle boot lying in the middle of the road several feet from the wreckage.

A man was running toward her and yelling, "He didn't stop! Drove right in front of me! Is he dead? Did I kill Cousin Billy!?"

While it was too dark to see who the man was, Emily would know that voice anywhere. It was Dex who had run into Billy's motorcycle in the intersection.

Winded, he finally reached her side and began trying to steer her back into the house. "We have to call 911!" he panted. "We have to get help, Emily!"

"Dex, what are you doing here?"

"I was worried about you. You just weren't yourself tonight, so I dropped Elaine at home and told her I left my cell phone at your house and had to go back for it. I wanted to make sure you were okay. We have to call for help now!"

Emily wasn't listening. She was watching the scene of the wreckage with awe. Grabbing Dex's arm, she said. "Hold on a second. Look." She pointed across the street and Dex's eyes followed.

He drew a sharp intake of breath and gasped, "What the hell is that? What's it doing?"

The black smoke was back. It had now fashioned itself into two huge musclebound arms, with hands the size of boulders, and was picking up the ruined remains of the bike and what was left of Cousin Billy. The smoke briefly twirled around the floating wreckage, totally enveloping it. Then the mangled motorcycle and Billy were gone.

45

Emily and Dex stared dumbstruck at what they had just witnessed. Moments later the boot disappeared from the middle of the road.

Emily uttered a small sob as she realized there were two disembodied, red glowing eyes staring balefully at her from the edge of her front lawn.

The disconcerting Darth Vader voice boomed, "Well played, mortal." It barked a thunderous laugh that shook the earth below their feet. Then it was gone.

In a small voice, Dex asked, "Em, what the hell was that?"

Emily swallowed hard and replied, "I don't really know, but I think it was Satan."

Dex looked at her with wide-eyed alarm. "Satan? Well what the hell did he do with the bike? And where is Cousin Billy?"

Emily took Dex's hand and led him inside. She hugged him and whispered into his ear, "There is no Cousin Billy, Dex. Remember? I made him up."

Catherine Turner is an award winning journalist and author. Her work has been featured in magazines and journals around the world. She is an animal rights activist and devoted wife and mother. She lives with her family and two dogs in Cork County, Ireland. Catherine attributes her gift of words to her frequent visits to the Blarney Stone.

Clicker Training

by Kellen Blair

CLICK. TREAT.

Click. Treat.

Click. Treat.

"It doesn't seem to be working."

"It's only been a minute. Give her more time."

Click. Treat.

Click. Treat.

"She's not even paying attention. She's going after her paw again."

"That's because you're not clicking fast enough. You need to keep her engaged."

Click treat click treat click treat click treat.

"She doesn't even want the treats now. Look at her. She barely has any hair left on that paw."

The animal trainer, hovering above them: "Clicker training takes patience. For the first few days, keep your sessions short and... oh Jesus!"

"Babe, can you hold her? I'll go get some wet paper towels."

"That's a lot of blood."

"It's her scab... she opened it back up..."

John and Jenny Woodhouse cleaned and bandaged their dog for the third time in as many days, then offered the trainer a cup of coffee. The trainer, a paunchy woman of sixty, took slow sips, an action that John misinterpreted as a hesitance to communicate. This wasn't the case. The trainer *was* communicating, had been for the last five minutes.

"Something's bothering her," the trainer said to the couple.

"You think?" John responded.

His wife elbowed him. "No need to be sarcastic."

"I'm sorry. Yes. She's anxious. Ever since we moved to this apartment. And we know… it's totally normal. There's an adjustment period. Our vet explained everything. We just…"

"We just want our Molly back."

The trainer took another slow sip of coffee. "She's not used to city life."

It was a statement, not a question, but John didn't notice. "No, she's not. We moved from upstate. But there's a park across the street. She gets a ton of exercise."

"And you've tried drugs."

"Everything. Prozac. Clomicalm. Doesn't work."

"And a new diet. And mental stimulation."

"We've tried all of that," Jenny said. "But she won't stop biting at that paw. Night and day… gnawing and gnawing and…"

"And we would just love somebody—anybody—to help us figure out why."

"I can understand," said the trainer. "And I wish I could be the one to do it. But for whatever reason, she won't tell me."

John produced a single bark of laughter, and then, following an uncomfortable silence: "You're being serious?"

"I'm not surprised that she doesn't want to confide in me. I train dogs for a living, so they see me as a teacher, not a confidant. To be honest, my specialty is bugs."

"Bugs?"

"Flies, gnats, the occasional spider. I haven't been bitten by a mosquito in twenty-seven years. One comes near me and I think to it, 'Not today bloodsucker! Feast elsewhere!'"

John nodded, stirred his coffee, glanced at his wife, then looked back at the trainer. "Silly me, I've just been using repellent."

Jenny kicked him underneath the table.

"But I have a friend from Chile staying with me this week," the trainer said, beginning to pack up her things. She threw clickers, toys, and treats that smelled of salmon into a giant tote; Molly was too busy biting at her paw to care one way or another. "Her name is Florencia Fernandez, have you heard of her?"

Jenny smiled. "Um, no. We haven't."

"She's quite famous. A regular on the talk shows. She once encouraged a beached whale off the coast of Mexico to wiggle his way back to the water. All while eating pancakes at a diner in Des Moines."

"Don't forget your coat," John said.

"I'll tell Florencia about Molly. She should be able to tune in, even from across town."

"That's very nice of you," Jenny said. "Thank you."

"Hopefully she can tell us why Molly is so scared. I'll call you tonight to let you know."

"We really appreciate it," John said.

"But no matter what she says, don't give up on the clicker training! It takes time but it really does work. Three or four sessions a day!"

"Sounds good. Have a good night."

〰〰〰

It wasn't until later, as she was taking a shower, that Jenny thought about what the trainer had said—about the word she had chosen. According to their vet, Molly was stressed, anxious, depressed. According to her friends in the dog park, Molly was confused, upset, homesick for the suburbs. Until today, nobody had ever suggested that their dog might be acting funny (if eating oneself alive could be described as funny) because she was "scared."

Jenny laughed at herself; she'd been scrubbing the same spot for almost three minutes.

⚜ ⚜ ⚜

Bzzt. Bzzt.

"Don't answer it," John said.

"Oh come on. You want to just ignore her?"

Taking a bite of his steak: "Yes."

"She thinks she's doing us a favor. I don't want to be rude."

"And I'd rather not listen to the batshit crazy dog trainer while I'm eating dinner."

"Well, fine, you win, it went to voicemail."

She dragged her fork through her mashed potatoes. John took another bite of steak. Molly, of course, picked at her paw.

Bzzt. Bzzt.

"She's persistent, isn't she?"

Bzzt. Bzzt.

"Well, go ahead and answer it."

"No, no, no" Jenny said. "I don't want to spoil your dinner."

Bzzt. Bzzt.

"Oh Jesus. Go ahead. If we make her mad she'll send a battalion of mosquitos after us."

"Too late, it stopped again. But for the record, you're not at all curious about what she has to say?"

"For the record, no, I'm not."

"You don't believe in telepathic communication with animals? Despite numerous accounts of it being a legitimate, helpful way of dealing with depressed pets."

"Somebody did some googling this afternoon."

Bzzt. Bzzt.

"For God sake."

"Well now I can't answer or she'll know I was just ignoring her before."

"You realize," he said, "that this is the definition of insanity, right? Trying the same thing over and over again and expecting a different result?"

"Or maybe whatever she has to say is just really important."

"Then she'll leave a message."

Jenny glanced at the screen of her phone. "She has. She's already left two."

The phone stopped vibrating, the caller once again sent to voicemail. A minute later Molly howled and Jenny knocked over her wine glass.

⚜ ⚜ ⚜

"Aren't you going to turn off your light?" John asked.

"Not sleepy yet."

They both stared at the ceiling. At the foot of their bed, Molly whined, scratching at the uncomfortable cone around her neck.

"Well, I'm sleepy. Do you mind turning off the light?"

"I'd rather leave it on for a few more minutes."

John exhaled loudly. "Because of those messages? You're actually taking them seriously."

Jenny turned onto her side, facing away from him. Of course she wasn't taking the messages seriously. But she was allowed a few minutes of feeling unsettled by them, wasn't she? Or was she supposed to share her husband's inhuman stoicism in the face of every disturbing experience? And "disturbing" was exactly the word for it. She wasn't frightened and she wasn't hysterical. She was disturbed, and she had every right to be. That high-pitched scream would've disturbed anybody, except maybe the robot lying next to her.

To her credit, she'd had a good sense of humor about the first message. She and John had even chuckled while listening to it.

Call me back as soon as you get this. It doesn't matter how late. Florencia's here with me now and she's tuned in to Molly as I speak. They've got a great connection. Lots to report. Please call back!

As they listened to the second message, their laughter took on a nervous edge, then disappeared entirely.

Please pick up. Molly can see you, and she can hear your phone vibrating, so I have to assume you're screening your calls. But please… you have to pick up next time. Something's in the house with you… Molly can sense it. She senses it and she's terrified.

John told her to delete the third message without listening; the last thing they needed was some lunatic dog psychic giving them nightmares. He was right, of course, so she smiled, and nodded, and pretended to delete it. Then, later, sitting on the toilet, she connected her headphones and listened to the third message by herself.

GET OUT OF THE APARTMENT!! IT'S DEAD AND IT'S IN THERE WITH YOU AND MOLLY CAN SENSE IT AND SHE… Oh God. It's walking into the dining room right now. It's only a few inches away from you. Molly can smell it. MOLLY CAN SMELL IT AND SHE'S SO SCARED AND SHE… OH JESUS CHRIST IT'S REACHING OUT TO TOUCH THE BACK OF YOUR NECK AND…

And what? The sentence was never finished, although someone with a poetic bent might argue that the trainer's piercing scream had provided a certain sense of finality to the thought.

So, yes, the messages had disturbed her. But that didn't mean she was taking them seriously. She wasn't sure if she believed in psychics or not, but she knew she believed in con artists,

and given the two options, the latter made more sense. Yes, the trainer had guessed that they were in the dining room, so what? It wasn't a wild prediction to make at six-thirty in the evening. She'd met a palm reader in Arizona who'd used similar tactics. It all sounded so incredible until you realized a fifth grader could make the same educated guesses.

Tonight was about getting them scared; tomorrow would come talk of Florencia's uncanny ability to exorcise ghosts, all for a very reasonable fee. Thanks but no thanks. Better to just block the trainer's number and forget the whole thing. That's what her husband would do, no hesitation. In spite of any other fault he might have, John was practical, you couldn't argue with that. So that's what she did; she blocked the number. No more phone calls from the nutty animal trainer and her telepathic sidekick.

It was the right move to make and she knew it. But still… she was allowed to leave the light on for a few more minutes. At least until she was done thinking about the way the trainer had screamed, and about the way Molly had howled, and about the fact that she knew (in her stomach if not her head) that those two things had happened

about a minute into the voicemail

about a minute after the phone had stopped vibrating

at exactly the same time.

"What are you doing?" John asked.

"What do you mean?"

"You never sit over there."

"Does it matter? I feel like eating on this side of the table tonight. Who cares?"

"I thought you liked to face the window."

"Well, tonight I want to face the door. It's not a big deal. Pass the guacamole."

John, a horror buff, was ecstatic to discover that *Night of the Living Dead* was on Turner Classics at nine o'clock. Jenny thought about suggesting something else; a comedy, a compromise, but as soon as John started popping the cheddar-flavored popcorn (an only-every-now-and-then snack), she knew the battle was over. So she was a good sport, she cuddled close to him, and she scream-laughed at all the right places. For ninety minutes she watched dead things reach out to touch living things.

"They're so slow!" John said. "How were people scared by this?"

"It's the way they just keep coming at you, no matter what."

"Yeah, but they're just dumb, lumbering idiots. Actually, they'd be kind of cute if they weren't trying to eat you. Like pets."

He stroked Molly, who was sitting on the couch between them. A few minutes later, the dog howled, and Jenny instinctively reached for the back of her neck.

"Sit." Click. Treat.

"Sit." Click. Treat.

"Sit." Click. Treat. "Are you seeing this?"

"Hey, that's great," John said. "I guess that psycho was right. About click training, at least."

"*Clicker* training."

"That's what I said."

"Hey, let's see what else we can teach her to do."

"Is that *Molly*?"

Molly chased a squirrel to the other side of the dog park and Jenny smiled the smile of a proud mama. "Watch this," she said, getting down on her haunches. "Molly, touch!"

Click.

Molly bounded over, pressed her nose against Jenny's open palm. The dog park people clapped.

"Molly, stay."

Click.

Jenny backed away several feet; Molly didn't budge an inch.

"And… touch!"

Click.

Molly jumped into Jenny's arms. Everybody laughed.

"Do you want Molly on weekends?" Jenny asked.

"Okay," John said halfheartedly.

"If it's a chore, don't bother. She can stay here."

"Whatever you think is best."

"I think she'd like to see you now and then. But it's up to you."

"It's just… Mia has a cat."

"Oh. Got it. Yeah, Molly can just stay here. That's great."

When John left, Molly tried to follow him out into the hall.

"Stay." Click.

Molly stopped, watched him go.

Nothing about the situation was "great," but it also wasn't nearly as bad as Jenny worried it might be. Molly was better, which made it possible to live in the apartment alone. Jenny didn't believe in ghosts, but even if she did, Molly's improved behavior was an "all clear" on the paranormal front, wasn't it? The hair on Molly's leg had grown back, concealing whatever scars the trauma had left behind. Pretty soon Jenny would forget all about the scars. *Out of sight, out of mind*, she thought. And even if that wasn't strictly true (because, really, there were plenty of things you couldn't see that you still thought about), the bad dreams were becoming less frequent. So maybe *her* scars were healing too. Not healing, but disappearing. Grown over by a thick coat of new memories. Tonight, even though there was a *Nightmare on Elm Street* marathon on FX, she and Molly would be watching *Bridesmaids*. So there.

"Coming up next, we'll be talking to world-renowned animal communicator, Florencia Fernandez. Don't go anywhere!"

Jenny put down her phone and looked at the TV. She had a strong impulse to turn it off. What was the point of blocking the loonies of the world on your phone, if you were just going to start inviting them into your house via live television? Turning off the TV would be the practical thing to do. But then again, the God of Practicality didn't live here anymore; she was done worshipping at His alter. Let Mia pay tribute for a while.

The heavily lipsticked host came back on the screen and said, "So, Mrs. Fernandez, you communicate telepathically with animals for a living. You must get some strange looks when you meet people at parties."

A laugh from the audience.

"Oh, yes," Florencia responded. "I'm used to the cynics. But let me tell you, their attitude changes when I help them save their little animal friends."

Jenny had expected the Chilean accent; even the thick glasses and the curly red hair checked out with the image in her head. What she hadn't expected was for this nutcase to look so calm and collected. It was more than just that, though; she actually seemed trustworthy, warm, like a favorite aunt.

Florencia started telling the beached whale story. This was obviously a crowd favorite, and Jenny could see why. What Florencia was saying was implausible, almost impossible, but what about the video footage accompanying the anecdote? Apparently Florencia had been live-streaming the whole event. On half the screen, the telepath, in a trance-like state, mumbled words of encouragement. On the other half of the screen, a whale—a whale that supposedly hadn't move in hours—began to inch its way back into the ocean.

The audience clapped wildly. Then the host played a montage of various testimonials. Cats had been "talked" down from trees. Lost rabbits had hopped their way to safety. Hamsters on the verge of death had somehow found the strength to journey on. If this was a hoax, it was a hoax of massive proportions. And if it wasn't a hoax…

Jenny suddenly realized how cold it was in her apartment. She went to her bedroom and put on a pair of slippers, Molly following to and from as if attached by a string. When she sat back down on the couch, she looked closely into the eyes of the Chilean woman on her television screen, and realized… everything was okay. Florencia Fernandez might not be a con artist, but that didn't matter. She'd never personally met or spoken to Florencia Fernandez, had she? All of that "communication" had come through the clicker trainer. The trainer was the con artist, not Florencia. The trainer probably didn't even know the famous animal psychic; she probably just dropped that name to give herself some credibility.

Jenny reached for the remote, ready to move on with her life. But then she noticed that the host was wrapping up the segment, and she thought, *what the hell, I might as well finish it.* If only to prove to herself that there was no reason *not* to finish it.

"We only have a minute, Florencia. But I have one more question for you. Someone in your profession must have some strange experiences. What's the most bizarre thing that's ever happened to you on the job?"

Florencia's eyes flicked toward the camera, making temporary eye contact with Jenny (or at least the illusion of it). "Yes," she said, "I've seen many strange things. The most bizarre? That would have to be the case of Molly, a small dog."

So the dog's name was Molly, Jenny thought, *so what?* A few months ago she'd seen a list of the most popular dog names in America and Molly was ranked number two. There were probably thousands of Molly's bouncing around New York City alone.

"Like many of my clients, I never met Molly. Her parents… they weren't receptive to what I had to tell them. I never blame people for feeling this way—especially in a case like this."

"Hm," said the host with an air of exaggerated fascination. "And what was going on with Molly?"

Turn off the television, Jenny told herself. *Right now it's still just a coincidence. A funny story you can tell friends in a few years. Turn off the television before it becomes more than that.* But she found herself unable to move, almost as if an invisible hand were holding her in place.

"I've never communicated with an animal who was so frightened. Animals, dogs especially, are very sensitive to stimuli of all kinds. Even what some people might call supernatural stimuli."

"Do you mean to say… dogs can see ghosts?"

"Smell, see, sense… it amounts to the same thing. And Molly was scared because this… this thing… was walking around her home."

The host gave a little shiver. "What did this ghost want?"

"It's not a matter of wanting anything. The kind of spirit I'm talking about… it's only a shell. Does that make sense? It wanders without intention."

"And is this spirit still bothering Molly?"

"I check in with Molly from time to time.

I'm with her now. She's very happy."

"Oh, well that's great. So… the ghost is gone?"

"No. It's in the room with her, even now. A few inches away. But Molly isn't scared anymore. That's what makes this case so bizarre. I've spoken to many animals who have seen spirits before. Dozens. But I've never seen a situation resolve itself quite like this. The spirit—there's no other way to say it—has been tamed."

"What do you mean by 'tamed?'"

"Molly's owner… she was training Molly using one of those clicking devices. Sit, click. Fetch, click. You understand what I mean?"

The host nodded.

"As I said before, these spirits… they're mindless, malleable things. So… while the woman trained her dog… well…" Florencia's mouth widened into a huge grin. "She sort of inadvertently trained this dead thing too."

There were a few muffled laughs in the audience.

"Let me get this straight," said the host. "This woman… she tells her dog to sit, and what? The ghost obeys the same command?"

More laughs from the audience.

"That's right. I know, it sounds ridiculous. It *is* ridiculous. That's why Molly doesn't feel threatened anymore. The whole thing… it makes her laugh."

❦❦❦

The host and Florencia said their goodbyes, the audience clapped, and Jenny… she stood up from the couch, picked up Molly and the clicker, and began to slowly back away.

"Stay." Click.

"Stay." Click.

In her bedroom, she threw a few shirts and some clean underwear into a bag. In the bathroom, she grabbed her toothbrush and a comb. She had no idea where she was going, but that was a problem that called for a little sunlight and some fresh air.

"Stay." Click.

"Stay." Click.

Holding Molly close to her chest, Jenny reached for the front door, pausing only long enough to shout over her shoulder,

"STAY." Click.

Stay! Yes, stay where you are, but what about… oh Jesus Christ… what about all of those times she'd said "touch?"

"STAY!" Click

"STAY!" Click.

And then she and Molly were gone, the front door closing behind them. Click.

Kellen Blair is the Drama Desk nominated co-writer of *Murder For Two*, a murder mystery musical comedy that ran for a year off-Broadway and has been touring internationally since 2014. In addition to writing for the theater, Kellen enjoys writing fiction and poetry. He teaches film and playwriting in New York City, where he lives with his wife and young son.

Open Grave

By Jay Seate

1890 – England

INSPECTOR EDGAR BASHAM, retired from Scotland Yard for more than five years, was feeling a bit giddy. Not only were his aches and pains somewhat soothed by the slow pace of life in his adopted rural village, but he'd recently solved a local crime rather handily. Basham wasn't psychic. He'd merely followed a hunch which had quickly led to poor Mrs. Donovan who had killed her abusive husband. But there was still a downside to his sleuthing history—

the questions about the Ripper case, and the need to explain to everyone that he had quite possibly been the only Scotland Yard detective who hadn't worked it.

A rapping at Basham's door interrupted his philosophical reveries. It was tentative, little more than a rattling gust you might expect from the hand of a female, but he knew very well who stood outside—Constable Fellows. As a result of bringing Mrs. Donovan to justice, Fellows came to Basham every time a child lost his bicycle or a woman misplaced her parasol. Relocating to the country had proven to be anything but dull. On this occasion, the constable came knocking before Basham had digested his morning poached egg and finished his cinnamon tea. He felt a bit like Doyle's Sherlock Holmes playing against the irrepressible Inspector Lestrade. If only he had been put on the Ripper case those many years ago.

The knocking persisted, a little more insistent this time. Finally, the better angels of Basham's nature prevailed. With some effort he rose to his feet. It seemed gravity would prove the final victor. Crossing the room, he pulled back the door's bolt allowing the annoying interloper to cross the threshold. "What could it possibly be this time, Lest...er...Constable? A stolen pair of ice skates or high button shoes perhaps?"

"Sorry to disturb you, Inspector," he answered sheepishly as he removed his hat.

Basham felt ashamed of himself. He hadn't meant to sound superior. After all, it was he who'd agreed to assist in the Donovan case, so if he was sought after, he had only himself to blame.

"It's this way," Fellows continued, his peppered eyebrows huddling together for momentary consultation. "A body has been removed from the cemetery, the old place on the hill at the edge of town."

It was a sorry state of affairs when not even the dead could rest, Basham thought, but at least the supposition had more interest than a lost and found conundrum. "Go on," he told Fellows.

"This disturbance could have happened as much as a week ago. No one goes to the old place anymore. Most souls are put down in the churchyard."

"How did you discover the disturbance?"

A villager sometimes climbs the hill to drink in private. After a few nips, he stumbled upon the opening." Fellows thought for a moment. "Guess the old sot is lucky he didn't fall in and break his neck."

"Who does the grave belong to?"

"It belongs to Mary Rose Singleton. She's been dead for nearly a hundred years. You might've heard the story."

"No, but I'm sure I'm about to," Basham said. "Have a seat, Constable. It's a bit early for spirits, but I'll bring in a pot of tea to keep your vocal chords lubricated whilst you enlighten me."

"Splendid of you to take a continued interest in village affairs, old fellow."

Basham raised his eyebrows at the patronizing remark.

It wasn't too early for spirits of the ethereal kind, as it turned out. Ghosts are the origin of everything that frightens people. They appear in the folklore of all societies. Mary Singleton was somewhat of a legend in the region. For those who liked such tales, she was a perfect revenant. She'd been betrothed to a British officer who'd sailed to America to fight in the War of 1812 and promptly gotten himself killed at the Battle of New Orleans. Mary had been so distraught over the news she poisoned herself with hemlock.

"Poor woman. Legend has it she'd been seen staring out one of her windows for days at a time, pining away for her officer. She would occasionally whirl about the room as if dancing with him, but knowing she was never again to be swept up in his loving embrace." Fellows offered his soliloquy as if he'd known her personally.

Small towns like their stories as much as their gardens and canned preserves, so rumors about Mary occasionally wandering the countryside in search of her lost love played well. Basham could guess that the tale grew new appendages with each telling. So now her remains, or what was left of them, had joined her wraith and given the old tale new life, so to speak. No apparent clues as to who might have exhumed the body were found at the gravesite. As strange as it may seem, grave-robbing was not a specific crime, but the incident would certainly jangle the nerves of those who'd spent the better part of their lives listening to stories about the woman who'd risen from the grave in search of her dashing officer.

Basham, who did not feel like a museum piece quite yet, agreed to climb the hillside and have a look. He asked to go alone so he could think without useless questions from Fellows. The old cemetery rested on the side of a hill too steep to farm. There was a pleasant view of the isolated town below, with its church steeple rising above the elms and the oaks. There were no fences or signs to sequester the graveyard from the outside world. All that remained among a few empty whiskey bottles and weeds were a hundred or so old stones to mark locations of final repose. Whoever tended the graves of these souls must have been long dead as well. Maybe superstition played a role given Mary's legend, for Basham knew a tale told long enough becomes easier to believe. He further knew most of the locals had little to do except repeat gossip, even if it was one-hundred years old.

Mary Rose Singleton's headstone was simple with no ostentatious words of scripture or poetic sentiment. Just her name and dates of birth and death, and one curious engraving; Seek no longer the beloved, it read. So forlorn, so sad and final those words and dates, nothing more to come, nothing more to add.

Basham guessed the desecration was only a day or two old for the dirt clods still held moisture. Remnants of the burial casket remained. He didn't dare descend into the hole for fear that what remained would give way under his weight. Instead, he got on his hands and knees

for a better look.

The lid's hinges in rotted wood had broken easily, giving access to the corpse. Small traces of clothing could be seen in the bottom of the box, but had deteriorated to the point of near non-existence. Basham guessed Mary's bones were held together by no more than a few remnants of leathery skin. He saw nothing that would give any indication as to whom the robber might be, but felt sure it wasn't merely a ghoulish prank by youngsters. The thief had been careful about not leaving footprints or other clues.

The day darkened. Basham shivered as the breeze ruffled his hair and whispered against his exposed skin. The trees swayed gracefully like dark ballerinas moving to a rhythm only they could hear. It occurred to him that all of us, the living and the dead, had shared the same wind, trees, and the elements of nature. We came from the same earth and our roots always reached down into it.

The village had only two churches, but five drinking establishments. A sign of the times. Basham stopped in one of the pubs to shake the haunting feeling his visit to the cemetery had inspired. He was surprised to discover the constable and his men had managed to keep the latest news out of the pubs this long. He would congratulate Fellows at the next opportunity.

Basham recalled a long ago stop in a Whitechapel pub after thwarting a perplexing attempt on one Mr. Pippin's life. On that occasion, he'd seen the truth of the murders as clearly as if they had been tea leaves floating in his pint of ale. He hoped for such a revelation again, but his arthritis had crept over him like an angry spider, suggesting a hot bath might be of more benefit than drink. He shambled out of the pub onto the cobblestone path. The remaining fragrance from flowers that lay in ruin along the path's borders reminded him of death's finality, as he turned toward his cottage thinking about

Mary Singleton. He looked upon the mystery of her missing body as a macabre game. It was a puzzle to assemble, a project to complete.

He reported his observations, or lack thereof, to Fellows, but he was titillated by who might want to commit such an abomination as to take the remains of the local legend. On his own, Basham decided to take an indirect route. He rented a carriage and visited the region's Hall of Records where he researched the Singleton family history. As far as he could determine, there were no Singletons living in the area, but he also discovered the family name of the British officer. It was Musgrove. And at least one Musgrove appeared to be currently residing in the village.

The next day, Basham sought out the residence of Mr. Jeremy Musgrove. The cottage was on the edge of town as well, not terribly far from the hillside cemetery. No one answered the door, so Basham proceeded to another modest cottage, the nearest neighboring residence, and tapped on its door. A tomcat eyed him with suspicion and then rubbed against his trousers. A round-face child looked out a window and studied Basham with equal trepidation.

"Muuum!" the child bellowed and disappeared. The door finally opened as an equally round-faced, stout woman appeared with the child, eyes wide with curiosity, clinging to her skirt. The tom, seizing his opportunity, ran past everyone's feet into the domicile's sanctuary.

Basham removed his hat. "Good day, Madam," he said with a reserved smile.

"What do you want?" The woman braced the door frame with a meaty arm, a gesture barring any thoughts Basham might harbor of entry. She smelled of flour and something else less pleasant he couldn't identify. He feared he was losing his fine tuning for such matters.

"If I might have a word. I'm trying to locate your neighbor, a Mr. Musgrove," he said pointing to the cottage up the road. "Do you know

58

where I might find him?"

"Are you the police?"

"No, no. Just a friendly visit."

The woman shrugged her shoulders as the child yanked at her skirt. She looked at the cottage next to hers as if Musgrove might suddenly appear. "A strange one, he is," she said as much to herself as to Basham.

"How so?"

"Comes in and out at all hours. Stays to himself. Sometimes we hear him singing. Not a bad voice mind you, but it disturbs the little ones."

Basham waited for more, but the woman only stared at him with suspicion. Then he said, "Has he lived there for long?"

"He come down from London about a year ago, I'm thinkin'. A writer, he said he was. Working on a chronicle of England's history, or some such— not that the subject of serfs and Kings ain't been done enough. We've barely exchanged a word since. Just a wave now and then."

The child had become bored and disappeared along with the cat. Basham didn't ask the woman if she'd heard about the disinterment of Mary Singleton's remains. He wasn't sure how far information of the current atrocity had traveled and didn't want to unnecessarily alarm the citizenry.

"Thank you for your time, Madam. I'll try to contact the gentleman another time."

The woman looked Basham up and down and her eyes widened. "You're the one what cuffed Mrs. Donovan, ain't you?"

Why deny it. "At your service."

"But you said you weren't a policeman."

"Retired. Just an ordinary citizen now."

"Ordinary, my arse." The woman tilted her head sideways like an inquisitive dog. "What you got on this Musgrove?"

Basham realized a bit of subterfuge would be necessary to keep this woman still. "The gentleman has lost a relative in London," he whispered conspiratorially. "He's quite possibly in line for a rather nice inheritance. I want to break the news quietly, you understand. I must ask for your discretion in this matter."

The woman's arm dropped from the doorframe and her fingers fluttered a bit with the prospect of such interesting news. "Oh, yes Sir, of course, Sir. Mums the word."

"That's the ticket. Again, thank you for your time."

The mother stood in the doorway as Basham walked away, until a child started crying somewhere within the house. As she closed the door, he turned and spotted a stain on the hemline of the woman's dress. Spilled milk spoiling, he'd wager. Thank goodness for small favors. He felt like whistling until he refocused his attention on Mr. Musgrove. In a village this size, most people knew each other's habits, or thought they did. But someone relatively new to the area such as Musgrove could be more autonomous. Basham knew the dust would not settle under his feet before the house-frau would be jabbering to her friends, but at least it would not reveal his true intention: to find out what the most recent in a long line of Musgrove's might know of Mary Rose Singleton's disappearance.

On Basham's way home on a road bordered by trees and hedgerows, he saw a cloaked figure standing ahead, her lower third covered by a thin layer of ground mist. Maybe it was the ominous starkness of a woman alone, or her posture, but he felt a knot of disquiet. The figure stood rigid and motionless until her head titled slightly as if puzzling over his approach, a vision that injected a chill of foreboding. He considered walking the extra distance to where she stood, but he no sooner had the thought than the woman turned and walked into a wooded area, practically vanishing before his eyes. Was it Mary, freed from her dark one-hundred-year-old tomb? Eyewit-

nesses to an event were notoriously unreliable. Was he beginning to see things as well?

That evening, Basham sat amidst the comforts of the few personal items he'd brought with him from London. He sipped a brandy and listened to his grandfather clock chime away the quarter hours, while pondering what little he'd discovered about both Mary Singleton and Jeremy Musgrove, and content in the knowledge that Fellows had no reason to intrude upon his contemplation.

He felt sure the descendent of Mary's betrothed was the most likely to shed light on his investigation. He planned to pay Mr. Musgrove a visit once it was late enough to catch him at home.

Twilight had deepened into night. Basham saw a light in the cottage as he approached. Reaching the door, he also heard the singing. He believed it a ditty from one of Gilbert and Sullivan's operettas. When he knocked, the singing abruptly stopped.

"Who's there?" said a voice within.

"Edgar Basham."

"State your business."

"It concerns your family tree, sir."

"My what?"

"If I could just have a word. It won't take but a moment."

The door opened far enough for the two men to take the measure of one another. Jeremy Musgrove was a handsome lad Basham guessed to be in his late twenties. Like his neighbor earlier, it was clear he did not want a stranger inside his lodging. The young man stepped out of the cottage and tersely asked, "Well?"

"I understand you moved here from London not so long ago. I too, left the city and am glad of it. Have you enjoyed your time here?" It was just idle chatter intended to make Musgrove more comfortable.

"Yes, I like it here very much."

"So do I. You don't have the privilege of fresh air in the city."

"I say, did you come to talk about nature, or is there something else."

"As a matter-of-fact, it came to my attention that you have roots here. Your forbearers came from here. I'm guessing that history enticed you back."

"What if it did?"

Time to get to the point. "There was an occurrence in the old cemetery a few nights ago I believe you can shed some light upon. A grave was disturbed. The grave of a woman who has a history attached to her name. Your long lost relative was—"

Musgrove snapped to attention like a military bugle had sounded. He held up his hand. "I know the story only too well."

"Are you willing to tell it to me, filling in the current details? I can see you're a fine lad, and if I can find out what happened, it may save official intervention."

Musgrave's lips puckered into a quizzical ellipse before his expression conferred a decision. "Come in, Mr. Basham."

❦❦❦

Most people want to share their secrets no matter how dark, given the right circumstance. This was the case with Mr. Musgrove. Although raised in London, he'd been fascinated by the stories his family weaved about his ancestry, especially the tale about his great-uncle going off to war across the ocean and the love he'd left behind. His family had made ghosts, or stories thereof, an integral part of their lives.

These tales were fodder for a lifetime interest in history and genealogy. Interest in Jeremy's family tree remained undiminished and eventually brought him to the little village he and Basham now shared. Fancying himself a future novelist, he managed to purchase a house where he could work with words in relative solitude.

Having succumbed to the lure of the most interesting branch of his family tree, his mission was to investigate a tale he had first heard on his grandmother's porch.

With this history as a backdrop, he bade Basham take a chair. As for himself, he wasn't ready to sit. Instead, he paced back and forth across the room while Basham followed his moves as if he were watching a slow moving tennis match. Jeremy Musgrove's story continued thusly:

"Several months after moving into this cottage, I began to see Mary. The sightings were usually as dusk approached, not the time of day one prefers to see a strange apparition nearing the house like some impoverished waif wanting to be taken in. With each sighting, she came closer. Mary must want inside the house, I thought, while at the same time I worried that her desires might be sinister. Judging by her hooded appearance that simulated The Grim Reaper himself, maybe she wanted someone to replace my great uncle. Could some malevolent force want to stretch forth its tentacles around me in a supernatural embrace? Could her goal be, God help me, possession?"

Basham's face involuntarily twitched because the description the young man had given was eerily similar to the person he'd seen alongside the road.

"I must confess I've never been lucky at love," Musgrove mumbled mostly to himself, looking a bit self-conscious.

"Oh?" Basham said.

"My opportunities have never quite equaled my aspirations." His words seemed to rake at his throat as he struggled to rid himself of them. "Love, for me, is some mystic, heavenly rapture I've never quite achieved."

"Ah," Basham said. Without a by-your-leave, he removed his Cherrywood pipe from the pocket of his overcoat, struck a match, sheltered its flame, and drew it to the tobacco, thinking the pause might provide Musgrove with a moment of respite.

"Through many depressing days and lonely nights with unanswered prayers and unrealized dreams, I have never found a suitable mate. In recent years, I've shied away from entanglements." Jeremy stopped pacing long enough to consider his words. The yellow light cast from a coal-oil lamp gave his face the hopeless, waxen look of a drunkard. "Given these visitations, I couldn't help but wonder if Mary was still wandering between the finite and eternity, still hungering from her loss."

Musgrove took another moment to stare glumly out the window that led to a lane that, in turn, led up a hill to the cemetery beyond. Then his pace quickened, his arms enveloping his torso as he strode from one side to the room to the other. Shadows cast by an oil lamp fluttered across the walls stalking his every move. Basham said nothing, waiting for more.

"You must understand, my emotions had turned topsy-turvy. I tried to write, tried to launch myself into another world, but nothing worked. My mind focused in one direction alone— toward Mary. Finally every creak sounded like a footstep. I could almost hear a shuffling at the front door. If I closed my eyes for a moment, all would be well, but still I wondered if a preordained dance summoned by a historical choreography kept me tied to a power that was asserting itself from beyond the grave."

Musgrove mopped his brow and continued, "Then came the evening when I sensed some extraordinary event was about to take place. I didn't dare look out the window for fear I might see something other than the ivy creeper against the windowpane. Perhaps some shadowy, pallid figure peering in. I attempted to guide my thoughts elsewhere. If I fell asleep, I felt certain I would feel a hand on my shoulder. Could this whole business conclude with my sanity slipping away? The fabric of my life was tearing apart like rotted silk and I seemed powerless to stop it. A creak in a floorboard told me Mary was near. She was lingering in the darkness. Was I about to feel the coldness of dead lips on my flesh, as if touched by her from the grave? Or something more spectacular, like skeletal fingertips hooking into my flesh and pulling me into some unimaginable place where my very soul would be imprisoned."

The man spoke as if in a trance. "If I had entered Mary's coffin, the atmosphere could not have been more oppressive. Every sight and thought seemed charged with sinister suggestions and an unpleasant tendency toward the macabre. Lying in bed in the dark, a desperate compulsion to do something rose in me. A strange notion engulfed me, one that could not be banished. I wanted no more nights forfeited to the unknown and decided what I must do."

Basham was entranced by young Musgrove's story. He knew what he was about to be told would add to Mary's legend beyond anyone's imaginings, and he too had become a follower.

Musgrove's eerie diatribe continued. "Before Mary had the opportunity to take control I decided to remove my curtain of fear by paying a nocturnal visit to the hillside cemetery. I half expected to see Mary's spectral presence standing next to the stones, observing my actions with a desperate yearning for that which had been taken from her. I labored at my task of unearthing Mary until I finally heard the sound of my shovel splintering wood. I scraped away as much dirt as I could, for fear the lid would collapse under my weight, and make a mess of Mary. I knocked the corroded lock loose and raised the lid on creaky hinges. They broke from the stress of being opened.

"Pushing the lid aside, I beheld what was left of the body, which wasn't much. Mary's apparition had certainly been more recognizable than her remains. Her bones would have fallen apart if not for the few strips of parchment-like skin. With her body freed to rejoin her spirit, I felt exorcised. I'd done what Mary wanted, for the time being. I carried her over my shoulder down the hill," Jeremy said matter-of-factly. "I'm telling the truth, Mr. Basham."

"Of course you are." Basham realized he'd been holding his breath. As Musgrove's tale gained momentum, the retired inspector noticed a rather sinister looking dagger sitting on an end table, suitable for opening letters, or for something far worse. He also realized the most interesting part of the story was yet to come. In a voice, soft yet steady as a mountain, the same coaxing voice he'd used on suspects for years, Basham asked, "Where is Mary now?"

Musgrove sighed purposefully. "Confucius says there's wisdom in patience. I'm waiting for Mary to tell me what to do next."

He motioned for Basham to follow. He did so with a slight bounce in his step, feeling anticipation with a thread of unease stitched through it. What a difference an adrenalin rush could make for one's aches and pains. On the way to an adjoining room, the inspector slipped the pointed weapon he'd spied on the table into his coat pocket. Better safe than sorry. The bedroom had a window that also faced the hillside graveyard. A figure sat there, curtains parted slightly.

A jolt shocked Basham's system. "Bloody hell," he breathed.

"There's a book I plan to write once the story concludes," Musgrove said. "Once our travail is complete. She's journeyed beyond the veil of death and found a place here at the window, earthbound again in body, sort of. It's not as if she can have the joy of life, but she can at least sit and survey the land she and her soldier were familiar with."

Basham approached the macabre spectacle at the window, treading lightly, as if approaching a living being. There was no odor of noisome decay. Mary was decades beyond that, but the normally ambrosial smell of lilac repelled him. With a little ingenuity using wire and adhesive, it hung together pretty well. She was adorned in a simple dress, for modesty's sake. The inspector could hardly imagine a more disparate combination—this young man obsessed with a virtual pile of bones.

"Now I can talk to her every day about this, that, or the other," Jeremy was saying. "That is something at least, having the company of a man who is in one piece. She's had to endure a century without company. I sing or whistle a tune now and then, thinking she might appreciate music."

Jeremy's perceptions were riven and the fault lines ran deep, but his passion rang true. His devotion to this legend had driven him quite mad. No doubt about that.

Seek no longer the beloved. The inscription on Mary's tombstone seemed hollow, for Musgrove had seen to it that her search had not concluded. Jeremy was convinced she was beckoning him to become her lover in her officer's place. Although her eye sockets were as empty as her grave, he believed she could see. Mary, the new mistress of his cottage was now in control. Musgrove carried a stain of his own, not on his clothes, but on his psyche.

For good or ill, no matter how bizarre or pernicious the behavior, there was always a motive for every action. That's not to say they are rational; they usually aren't. Somewhere Basham had read that insane people thought themselves sane. They often didn't fight their affliction because there were pleasures and beauty in madness. Basham would try and see to it that Musgrove was provided comfortable accommodation back in London where his illness could

62

be treated. His separation from Mary Rose Singleton would be difficult, but like most obsessive relationships, the path to perfection seldom runs true.

But what of Basham's own observations? The chill of the cemetery? The woman up the road? Was the phantom image and Mary's remains connected? And there was something else he hoped would amount to no more than a case of forgetfulness. Upon returning to his own cottage, he noticed something different about his chessboard, which served as display more than gamesmanship. The black queen had leapfrogged its protecting pawns and stood on a center square, ready to do battle with the white kingdom. Had he mindlessly placed the piece there? If not, who or what?

Perhaps we make our own ghosts. In the end, he decided he'd become much too impressionable for his own good.

Jay Seate is a writer who stands on the side of the literary highway and thumbs down whatever genre that comes roaring by. His storytelling runs the gamut from Horror Novel Review's Best Short Fiction to the Chicken Soup for the Soul series. His memoirs and essays report fact, while his fiction incorporates fantasy, horror, or humor featuring the quirkiest of characters.

Telemachus Press, a unique author services company and proud sponsor of *Who Knocks* magazine.

- **You keep all rights**
  - **You keep all royalties**
    - **You keep control of your work**

Call or email us today for a *free* consultation!

(941) 504-5496
Info@TelemachusPress.com
www.TelemachusPress.com
www.BookPubNow.com

TELEMACHUS PRESS

64   Image copyright iStockPhoto/ 146882475/ stoupa

Family Matters

BRIDGITTE LESLEY

Meryl was prepared to make the long trip to move from the busy bustling city to a ranch in the middle of nowhere. A total career change was not only welcome but something she needed. Life had thrown her a curve ball but she would bounce back.

Ray didn't think he would get a response from his advert he had placed in a magazine for a house-keeper. The one and only response he got was the person he appointed.

After days of travelling Meryl arrived at the ranch but minutes later she changed her mind and left. Ray had to make quick work of calming the waters. He didn't want to let her go! They seemed to have their wires crossed. She returned to the ranch and flourished in her new role as Ray's house-keeper. Little did they know what the future held for them on the wide expanse they called home.

Available on Smashwords.com